T0146771

A Dirty Game

Wilfred Ndum Akombi

Langaa Research & Publishing CIG
Mankon, Bamenda

Publisher:
Langaa RPCIG
Langaa Research & Publishing Common Initiative Group
P.O. Box 902 Mankon
Bamenda
North West Region
Cameroon
Langaagrp@gmail.com
www.langaa-rpcig.net

Distributed in and outside N. America by African Books Collective
orders@africanbookscollective.com
www.africanbookcollective.com

ISBN: 978-9956-579-70-9

One

Sitting and sipping spirits with friends of the same political party and discussing the possibilities of becoming richer was a pastime for Foti. He, like his friends, had a huge appetite for riches and hated to discuss with any low class men in society, as birds of the same feather flock together.

People often thought he was the architect of hideous and incredible acts because he wasn't open in whatever he was doing. It seemed none of his convictions in all his life would ever quash those allegations. Foti was the Lord Mayor of Tiko. He fought hard for the position and was fighting hard to maintain it. The people of Tiko city gave him many names: obstinate fellow, political sphinx, financial wizard, big fish, quiet killer, unscrupulous mayor and so on.

It was bright that afternoon. The mayor was ready to address the people on the death of former mayor, Kamso. It was one of the biggest crowds with almost all hands on jaws. Kamso died just two days before, on January 1st, 2010, on his way from a New Year party. Before his death, he had become a well known face in Tiko. He was a member of the opposition party thrown out from the council after a parliamentary political duel.

'Crime in this area is on a marathon increase,' said Foti to the crowd. 'It is a point of concern for every Tiko man in particular and the entire Southwest region as a whole. I will not hold my breath for a second until those who have assassinated the former mayor are brought to order. The forces of law and order are seriously investigating...'

The population was in chaotic voices that Saturday morning. It should be recalled that Kamso had designed an excellent plan for Tiko subdivision during his five years as head of the council. In the midst of the crowd were journalists from private newspapers as well as human rights activists. When the mayor stepped down from the elevation after his speech, many journalists scrambled to question him.

'Lord Mayor,' said Tanga, a most popular journalist.

'The people do not know how the deceased was dealt with. Do you have any word of explanation?'

'Ehmm ehmm… I was informed thirty minutes after the incident. I reached the scene five minutes later and saw blood oozing from the deceased's skull. For now, I have nothing to say about how he was killed until the investigations end.'

'His death has come just at the time of allegations of attempted murder on the late mayor by a group of militants from your own party. If you can see on the placards held by some of the people in the crowd, it is written that militants of your party killed the former mayor. How do you react to that?'

'Such allegations by The Watch Newspaper aren't true. There was a thorough investigation. Our militants were not involved in such malignant acts. I think any allegations could carry tremendous consequences if they can not prove it. Any assassination of character shall be redressed in the court of law.'

'*The Watch Newspaper* once reported that he escaped assassination in a previous incident, and no accusation of false statements has been made. Last week, there was another report that *Silence is acceptance*. Is that true?'

'No. Let *The Watch Newspaper* and its opposition-sponsored bunch of political maniacs say whatever they want. I think we are in a country that operates on law like any other. Let them baffle us in a court of law if they're confident in those allegations.'

'Some of the militants…'

The mayor suddenly tore through the crowd, leaving Tanga and other journalists. The police guarded him to his jeep. He adjusted his gowns on his shoulders with a fat and courageous smile and entered the ostentatious car.

Foti was very close to Kingsley Ebot, the police commissioner for the subdivision. Through Kingsley, Foti commanded the Tiko Police even more than the divisional officer who had that right more than all others. The ruling party, the CPDM (Cameroon People's Democratic Movement), controlled Tiko Subdivision. The majority of sympathisers of the main opposition party in the country, the SDF (Social Democratic Front), were English speaking Cameroonians. Meanwhile, the majority of CPDM militants were French speaking.

The opposition party had been and was the main political impediment for Foti in that local government area.

Two

In the city, a demonstration formed spontaneously. Men, women, and students didn't take long to make placards with such writings asking for the mayor to account for Kamso's death.

The sun was setting and secondary school students with some university students from Buea started putting houses into flames. They had been accumulating anger for long.

At the greatest dilemma, Foti called the commissioner of police.

'This is a grave situation,' he said.

'What do you think?' asked Kingsley in an eager response.

'Send your boys to stop those rowdy cowards. The next target could be my villa.'

Kennedy, the mayor's son, a calm and gentle man, came with words that the crowd was making way for the State Counsel's fabulous house. A call came from the Divisional Officer asking Kingsley to join police officers with gendarmes to stop the crowd from destruction.

Tanga was actively rushing after the crowd picking all events. That was his job and he always proved that he loved it. It wasn't only because of money but because he found solace in it and was hugely dedicated.

Like frightened palm birds, the students retreated from the council building, rushing towards the municipal stadium. The gendarmes fired their first shot in the air.

Bergit was a Doctorate student pursuing his career in constitutional law. He had been with his supervisor, Professor Hansel, for two days working on his thesis for a final defence. He lived in Tiko while following studies at the Buea University.

A police truck was on high speed from the direction of Public Security. They were chasing the crowd. With them were water cannons, tins of tear gas, guns, police knives, and other lethal weapons.

Bergit was not aware of the gravity of the spontaneous demonstration and reckless approach of the police. He could not turn to escape but to approach the truck when he saw it from a distance. With greatest dexterity, a police officer was holding the bar behind the truck with his left and his gun in his right hand. He fired twice on the forehead of Bergit, as he approached.

His brain oozed out like some rubbish kind of a thing. The watching crowd wailed from a distance and then disorganised. Bergit fell on his file full of papers. Brown ground suddenly turned red.

The truck moved a little. 'Don't move,' said a police officer to a secondary school boy frightened by the sound of the gun. He walked to the boy. 'Stand on your head, you yam,' he shouted. 'You're one of those throwing stones at the police.' Then, he shot the boy on his belly. His stomach cut into two and his intestines bundled out. The students yelled from a distance and disappeared.

In his car, the Divisional Officer drove slowly from behind with two gendarmes guarding him.

In front of the municipal hall were placards dropped by the escaping crowd. There were many writings on them: 'enough is enough,' 'the mayor must account for Kamso's death,' 'Why continuous increment in university fees?' 'The mayor should be hanged for crimes against humanity,' 'Taxes gotten from Southwest petrol should be for local Limbe council than to the capital city,' 'God, help your people from the agony of hunger,' 'No more destruction of our forest by Europeans,' 'China must be fair in trade than free in trade.'

The Divisional Officer climbed down his trendy car and stood looking at the council hall in flames. 'This is the good works of the opposition.' said the officer to his assistant and guards. The aged man supported himself with an oak walking stick, appearing like a don of a mafia group. He walked steps ahead. His assistant caught sight with the body of Bergit. They walked and stood beside it. 'This is just one of the ways to surmount this devastating state of affairs,' he said pushing the body with his leg to confirm he was dead.

'I suppose more troops be sent from the capital city,' said the commissioner of police.

'That's right,' supported the DO. The police truck wheeled back from behind the municipal stadium. The bad news that a university student was dead hit all corners of the Subdivision and the National territory. The family screamed rushing to the scene. The deceased's mother stumbled on the corpse and lied on it unconscious while other family members were bulldozing dust in screaming voices. Coincidentally, the police met the deceased's family in that fumbling disappointment.

'Let's get them arrested,' shouted an Inspector of police.

More police officers and gendarmes stormed the scene arresting many others- both young and old, men and women. Tiko was in disorder that evening. Ears were upright and radios all tuned to get full details of such devastation.

* * * *

Bakwa FM was the most popular of all private stations. It had been banned twice. It was only when allowed to be monitored by the general manager of the lone government radio and television, that it continued operation. Tanga was one of its popular veterans. He was an eloquent journalist known both home and abroad.

That evening, Foti sat in the sitting room, sipping from his wine glass and his left hand on his wife's thigh. He seldom drank wine but could die for strong spirits, which he was becoming addicted. Because of his serious heart problems, his physician advised him on several occasions, that he risked losing his life.

His two sons stood outside near the garage discussing with two ladies. Their laughter gave an impression that the family was breaking even.

'You see what I say,' said the Mayor. His wife didn't respond. She continued flipping television channels and humming a song.

'Please,' said the mayor, 'call in Williams and Kennedy.' Abiga heaved to her right and picked up a telephone. With it, she called her two sons, though she could hear them talk. They opened their cars and the two ladies sat in.

'Sit all of you,' he ushered. 'There's one thing I have to tell you.'

'Yes, Dad. What's it?' asked Williams.

'The life of a politician is like that of a snake during a sunny day in a rainy season. The sun shines bright and it soon pours. If a green snake fails to bask itself in the least sun, it could miss it for the whole day.' He coughed and sipped twice. There were doubts articulated on various faces.

'What then, Dad?'

'I mean you all have to utilise this opportunity to experience financial growth. Suppose I'm kicked out from this position. Know that politics is the most unpredictable thing one can ever imagine. Don't just be contented with the small businesses.'

At some length, none of them said a word. 'I'm sure you get the rumours about how much the honourable MP has in his foreign account.' Still, none of them responded. He raised his head to Kennedy.

'You do, Ken.'

'Yeah.'

'How much is it you hear?'

'Nine hundred million…'

'That should be your thinking. He has bought a villa in Paris. Think big now or suffer when I am no more. This is the time to move mountains.'

8

As he talked with his sons, BAKWA FM radio was on. Music had been emanating. It was 8 pm and was top hour news time.

Mayor Foti was never a fan to BAKWA FM, but his wife was a devotee due to the good quality of BAKWA music. The sound suddenly stopped.

'It's 8 pm,' said the journalist at the anchor. 'It's news time and in our major stories:

University students have taken to the streets.

ASSIGOV to help poor governments pay debts.

The news in details; Following the murder of the former mayor for Tiko Subdivision, students took to the streets this evening asking the incumbent for an account. The police and gendarmes stormed the scene and shot two students dead. Tanga followed that story and now reports.'

'Hundreds of students, hundreds of policemen… As if guns have become play things of the 21st century…'

Lights suddenly ceased. There was a black out for about thirty minutes. When things came to normal, only music again was emanating from BAKWA FM radio.

Foti was in greatest doubts what details were in the news when the lights ceased. Kennedy and Williams were off to their various apartments. He whipped his mobile telephone and dialled the commissioner of police.

Commissioner Kingsley had always warned that Tanga was an unpleasant element. Their hatred for Tanga had not grown to a higher level over the years, but Tanga's questions to Foti during this particular interview arouse more concern.

'Lord Mayor,' said Kingsley, 'that's what I have been saying about the opposition party. They spend time sponsoring people to monitor us than follow the rules of politics. We've got to swiftly slug it out.'

'Who is Tanga? A child picked from the gutter. We have to eliminate him. I swear to my God.'

That night, Tiko Subdivision was completely dead. Only wind rattling tree leaves and the buzzing voices of police and Gendarmes that one could hear.

Private papers were fast to produce cartoons of the police shooting at students, and the mayor holding a pistol.

Early the following morning, *The Watch Newspaper* was selling more than ever before. There were headlines such as; Who Killed the Former Mayor? A PhD Student Gunned down By a Reckless Policeman. A Secondary School Student Breathes no More.

The newspaper sold that morning like wild fire. The news was quite miserable.

Foti woke up when the morning was aging out. In his trendy Volkswagen car, he patrolled the city, so disdainful in look. Perhaps, just to study the environment and peoples' reactions. At the heart of the city, he dropped. He could see those who mattered in that neighbourhood reading newspapers. He walked a little, this time alone, and saw some of the papers thrown away. He picked up one and saw a caricature of himself strangulating the former mayor. People watched him from a distance. Foti jumped into his car and negotiated towards the Commissioner's. At the police station, he descended with commanding steps like a military captain on duty.

'Good morning, King,' he said to Kingsley.

'Lord,' Kingsley responded beckoning him to a seat on his right.

'The news is rumbling like thunder…What's your thinking?'

'Tanga and some of his mates should be eliminated.'

'For sure, but it must be tactical and swift.'

'Right, but how does that work?'

'Use your boys, Kingsley.'

'Not my boys. It's complicated at this level. Forget my constables and get some of these brutes around involved.'

10

They were in low voices. A police constable entered expecting his boss to give him room to lay his complaint. For several seconds, he stood there unheeded while Kingsley seriously searched for a telephone number on his phone.

'Sir…,' said the constable.

'What?'

'This is a note from the State Counsel asking for the release of family members of one of those shot yesterday.'

'What! Was the family arrested?'

'I doubt. Maybe…' fumbled the constable. Foti was obstructed.

'Just get to the cell and ask. If not available, get to the gendarmerie and hand it to the *Commandant.*'

The constable dashed off.

Kingsley communicated with Obi Dialo who lived at the regional headquarter of Buea. In some two hours, Obi entered the commissioner's office. Foti was off but would return soon.

'Is there business?' asked Obi.

'Yes, something bigger just like that of last time.'

'What's that?'

'Do you know Tanga? I think you do.'

'You mean the journalist?' he asked with a little cruel and bold smile.

'Right… He has been following up with the last incident step by step. If we don't eliminate him, we could be discovered. Even you too won't be safe and you know it good.'

'We need to talk with the mayor then.'

'He'll be here in a jiffy.'

Obi was a boy of gigantic and frightful muscles. His eye colour was dirty brown. His funny structure could frighten even a wild animal; a hunchback, overgrown bushy hair, K-legs, dirty dark in complexion, rough beard, and of a considerable height.

Foti re-entered and said to Obi, 'Thank God you're here. Did you come by helicopter?' he joked.

Obi smiled perfunctorily and said, 'How and why do I hesitate when you need me?'

'Alright gentleman, good you know that. Has Kingsley hinted you on the issue?'

'Yes.'

'Good. I'll settle you the way you want. Make sure nothing should be heard of him. Do it and leave no traces.'

Obi was a swift man in actions. He didn't waste a second to talk about the price. 'Five million now and five after execution,' he proposed.

'That is no problem,' responded Foti signing a cheque. 'Get it in full. I know success is visible just like last time. I trust you.'

'Thanks for the confidence. You need not squander your breath the least. Reserve it and consider the job done. Give us just a week. We'll study him, where he lingers at leisure time, and we'll trap him.'

Obi was rare on public occasions. This was because he was living a defensive life. He had secret friends from all over the region. One of Obi's friends was Ashu Ngo. He was from Tiko residing in Buea. Ngo was a school dropout and one of the two sons of a police constable, Grace Asong, working at the regional Headquarter.

Obi left for Buea. They would camp same evening for plan of action.

Tanga was hard to study. He had worked with Cameroon Radio and Television for two years as a senior reporter, but was relegated of his post to a simple clerk. The reason he abandoned the lone government station and joined BAKWA FM. He had suddenly become rare on the streets except when covering an event.

Ngo had known Tanga some two years back during his secondary school days. He equally knew a story about Tanga and one Esther Bih, at this time a restaurant manager.

Tanga had promised to have Bih's hand in marriage but shattered her heart when he fell out from Cameroon Radio and Television.

On her part, Bih tried to kill Tanga with poisoned food on two occasions but failed. It was for this reason that Tanga desisted from eating in public restaurants.

A week passed. Ngo couldn't take back any good news about the modus operandi to wipe Tanga. He thought of Bih, the failed marriage, and the attempted murder on Tanga. He was eager to talk to her so as to get some more information.

It was Sunday morning. Christians were on the streets, on their way to various denominations. Ngo took off for Bih Restaurant.

'How is Buea?' Bih asked.

'Things are disorderly in order.'

'What do you mean?'

'I mean just the political upheavals and the desperation.'

'It's everywhere.'

'I hear Tanga is digging it out with the mayor and his councillors.'

'Yes. The fool claims he wants to dig everything out. But he forgets to know how dangerous the mayor is. The mayor is a smiling man on his face but has continues tears in his heart when it comes to political obstruction.'

'Is he married?'

'Can the idiot get a wife? He keeps deceiving girls around. Didn't you hear? He said I wanted to poison him because he failed to take my hand in marriage.'

'I heard such rumours but I was not really sure of its veracity.'

'I'll kill him first… Let's wait and see,' she said.

'Good. I didn't just want to dive to it without knowing your mind. Let me leak this secret to you. Tanga hopes to see you dead. You know the scandal goes on and many people around this place look at you now to be a villain. Many people consider you to be a very nasty woman, although they can't say it to your hearing.'

'Not me. I'll do all I can. I'll sleep on graves and talk with the dead people just to see him dead... He is a rogue not me.'

'It's hard,' interrupted Ngo. 'One hardly sees him in public except when all eyes are on him. I mean when he is covering an event.'

'Not actually. The imbecile sleeps at Che Hotel. He thinks that it's the safest place on earth.'

'Occasionally?' Ngo asked with lots of concern.

'The childless coward sleeps there often, except when out of station.'

* * * *

Che Hotel was in a small town, two kilometres from Tiko. It was one of the few places to lodge, considered having some considerable security at the local level. If not out of the hotel or through the security, it was tough to penetrate. From the highway to the hotel building, one would pass through a garden of wild flowers. It was a distance of just one hundred metres.

Ngo left Bih. She didn't know that he had pulled the wool over her face, just to get Tanga's foot path and to deal with him first. Even if Ngo had revealed to her that he was out to put Tanga's life in peril, she would have still been happy to say it all. However, Ngo wanted to be sure that after their mission, there would be no traces, so that it would be hard to investigate.

When Ngo left to meet Obi and friends, he was sure that a visible success was just ahead. During that week, the mayor greased their efforts with a promise of doubling the amount if they gave Tanga an instant burial. Yet, it wasn't successful that week.

Daily, at 5 am, Tanga would leave the building and walk between the flowers to his Mercedes car, then for the station, or chasing a scene of activity to capture for a report.

The mayor's life was under intimidation. He received letters from unidentified persons stating that he and his family would not exist for having a hand in the deaths of his predecessor, two students, and many others.

Meanwhile, feeble investigations were going on. Still, critics described it as a ploy to delay and wipe the dirty file. Thus, his two sons became sceptical and were too rare at home and also on the streets.

Coincidentally, Williams decided to be passing the night at Che Hotel while trying to execute a contract awarded to him by the Tiko council to electrify two villages. He was also awarded a contract to immediately reconstruct the destroyed Tiko community hall. For fear of easy identification, Williams changed his car. He bought a Mercedes car. He would leave the hotel between the hours of five and six in the morning.

Three

Obi and his friends were determined to make it that Monday morning. They were in a yellow taxi, the colour of all Cameroon taxis. They were massively in disguise- only their eyes could be seen.

At 4.30 am, they hid in the bushy flowers that surrounded the hotel, all with pistols, poised to shoot at the veteran.

William's car was parked at the front parking place, while Tanga had come late and parked his car far off from the main entrance.

Both men were of considerable heights. Tanga loved sober suits, so too Williams. All description about Tanga was clear. They thought they knew whom they wanted to kill and they were sure to do it.

It was exactly five, but still as dark as a dungeon. They had been waiting for half an hour, balanced to take action. Williams walked gently towards his car. He perceived the tang of a strange perfume. 'Is it a devil wearing this kind of body spray or a human being with this hazardous smell?' he wondered. But that was not his business.

Ngo bent behind William's Mercedes car, ready to fire. His friends were about three meters away seriously watching. Williams stretched his hand to open his car. Obi cued with a sharp whistle like a chirp by a cricket. Ngo fired twice on Williams.

He fell beside his car, suffocating and blood oozing his chest. He mumbled and blood foamed from his mouth. 'I knew this would hap... hap...' Those were his last words. At this time, they began to pull him into the car.

Tanga was behind time. He didn't take the path through the main entrance, but another path between flowers, formed by children doing hide and seek. From that end, he edged his car into traffic. He couldn't accelerate fully when he saw a man tugged into a car. He speeded towards it to see clearly. They all escaped but then firing from the flowers, perhaps to scare him off the scene. He idled for a few seconds. They immediately spread his car with bullets, but he galloped on stones towards the hotel through the main entrance hitting on trees and his car rattling the flowers.

The shock and a bullet on his right arm weakened his nerves. He surrendered the steering seriously damaging the car.

Security men heard the heavy noise. Without any waste of time, they swooped to the scene. For the length of ten minutes, they tried to revivify him while rushing him to the hospital. Until they reached the Tiko District Hospital, Tanga was wordless, only his heart was beating.

On their way back, they saw and identified the body of Williams. It was hair raising and unbearable. It was incredible breaking news. When they rushed it to the hospital, the doctor on duty confirmed that he was dead.

* * * *

Mayor Foti was high-tempered. He would react and only reason several minutes after the act.

The body of Williams had been registered and left at the mortuary. When Security Chief informed the police, Kingsley didn't waste a second to give Foti a call. At first, he didn't tell him that his son was dead.

'Williams is seriously injured and has just been rushed to the hospital.'

'Are you serious about that?'

'I mean it. It is fifty percent death and fifty percent life.'

Kingsley didn't want the *heart attacking* news put Foti to a comma. He knew that in such circumstances, Foti would always react cowardly. He also feared that Foti's heart problems, which he had been having over the years, would develop into something bad.

When Foti saw the corpse, things turned sour. It was bad news indeed.

'My son gunned to death! Oh, God, my son?' he cried venomously. 'These are intrigues to dismantle all I have constructed in my life. However, this is a war without end. This is just the beginning. Let people be ready to fight now.'

On his part, Kingsley tried to calm him. Foti was in tears. He cried hitting his chest, moving forward and backward. 'Except I'm not Foti, I'll do the undone.' He roared as a strongest lion challenged in its den by a goat. 'I am going to edify this society.'

He punched the air and then slapped the wall. This time, he was like going out of his senses. People gathered to convince him that such a thing was part of life.

The deceased's mother didn't succeed to reach the hospital. She fainted at the main entrance and was brought in on a stretcher, and was soon on a hospital bed.

Foti was never flippant in words. He preferred to lament after action than never act at all.

* * * *

The former mayor was no more and there was no serious investigation into his death, many had criticised. A PhD student and a secondary school student had been shot dead too. This time, it was the mayor's own son. 'It has gone beyond normal,' the Commission of police said. 'I'll demonstrate my talent.'

Kingsley was sure the murderers would be trapped down. When he and his constables reached the scene, they found a gun. Kingsley was convinced that the gun belonged to another police officer. He was sure that it could help in the investigations.

After Foti wept for several minutes, a chilled thought flowed from his head down. 'What coincidence that Tanga was in same hotel!' Those thoughts pursued him right to his house.

In his glad days, he would wallow in comfort in a swivel chair. This time, it was only pain and tears flowing from the eyes of a responsible man. 'I'll avenge the death of my son no matter what it takes,' Foti cried. 'His hands are clean. I shall not wait for any retribution. I shall recompense myself.'

When one day counted off, the ugly news hit the entire region, with papers sold at random.

However, investigations had started. Criminal police officers of the whole Southwest region were under supervision for serious investigations.

Meanwhile, the serial number of the gun was faxed to the regional police. When the feedbacks were gotten, there was dread how the pistol could be found at such devastating scene. The pistol was identified and the owner too, Grace Asong, a police constable. Her file was spotless of felonies and even misdemeanours. She had had no single simple offence in her life. Her file was clean. But what misfortune befell her? No one seemed to tell then.

A week more counted off but no police officer reported of a missing gun as the police expected Grace to do.

Tanga had recovered and statements taken from him. He wasn't aware that the assassins aimed at him but missed their target.

Four

A week after the investigations into the dead of Williams, the family of Bergit decided to lay him to rest. At the solemn occasion near the grave, family members said final words.

Professor Hansel walked forward lackadaisically holding an epitaph. In that agony, Hansel couldn't manage himself. He held the four full scraps of paper but his head rose. Like he wanted to make a point before reading the epitaph, '...Bergit Adamu was the most compliant student I ever supervised. He was unique in academics. The more, he had become a friend and a brother to me. The same day he was killed, we concluded his thesis, a work he is supposed to present next month to end his long and tough career, to become an honoured PhD holder.

When we heard that the street was on fire, Adamu didn't say a word. He didn't care about the streets. But now, he lies like history, speechless.'

Hansel sighed, blinked and squeezed his eyes. Others supported him. He gathered himself and raised the paper to read the epitaph. Still, his hand fell. Something was on his lips. He didn't want to continue reading.

'Youths of this country,' he said, 'political lunatics have turned our natural resources into money for purchasing lethal weapons to consolidate their political stance. He was an enterprising young man who is no more. The forces of law and order have decided to do that. If not in your own country, where do you find solace? If protection does not come from the forces of law and order, from where do we get that? Youths, let's rise in one accord to face these political challenges. Let's face the storm in various ways.'

People continued to nod heads with wet eyes. The grey man's nostrils became watery.

'My children,' he continued in tears, 'if your neighbour is attacked, take a breath for you might be the next. I have been to European countries and to America. There's no sanctuary there as most people think. About eighty percent of the African working population there are toilet and restaurant cleaners, if not asylum seekers packed in small containers. Through the Sahara to Europe for greener pastures, many young people have disappeared. Why all these? This is because of the storm. Let not this irritation shove you out of your place of abode. I want to tell you that home is home. It necessitates you to combat all odds in your home so as to make it a better place to live. Never taking on arms but overcoming temptation, diligent in your daily convictions, pressing them down by your ability of goodwill nation reconstruction. You should know that triumphant songs come as a result of a just course. Let us not run away from this police recklessness but suppress by teaching them what a police officer is suppose to do.

I must warn you that our government and police officers are not yet mature enough to handle such crucial things as strikes. So, be careful the way you take to the streets. Please, abstain from those brutal acts like throwing stones at the police. The only response will be to shoot at you.'

Hansel paused a little when his wet eyes caught those of the deceased's father. 'Let the blood of Adamu journey the wishers to the darkest abyss, than yank them from their ruts,' he said poetically and spontaneously in suffocation. At this point, the musical set was switched on and a sorrowful mantra he had chosen gradually began to emanate. Some people also began to hum it. It was just a way to cover up the professor's confused emotions.

It was incredible that the ministry of higher education was hands-off the death. The higher education office had sent no word. When Hansel made mention of it, most family members motioned their open hands up, looking up the sky, like surrendering all things for the High Heavens to take control.

He had contributed a special coffin. In addition, he had written a farewell song.

The Pastor quoted from the Bible and then prayed. It was time for Adamu to take on his journey. The mantra CD was changed and the farewell song began. At the end of it, sorrows didn't let the professor read the prepared epitaph. They lowered the body and he walked towards the hall meant for them. Associate Professors and others who mattered followed him.

The deceased's enlarged picture was hung near the door. The promising man in an optimistic smile was in graduating robes, a picture when he was honoured with a master's degree.

Hansel starred at it for several seconds and turned to those behind him. 'Why should we stand to see the nation's dream evaporate? How shall we walk at age?' At this time, the poetic mind suddenly became ten years older than his age.

Tanga was there and his eyes were glued on every step taken by all. He was more and more becoming a political obstacle to Foti. He had not still understood that William's death would have been his.

The environment was solemn. Everyone had a sad look and dust would be hard to settle.

Hansel entered the hall and sat with other high-class men. There, were Primary school Headmasters, Principals, retired clerks, faculty clerks, writers and others. After the committal song, song after song kept the place funky.

'The century might be worst than any other history has ever registered,' said Hansel.

'What…' doubted an associate professor, Tabi.

'This is a century that seems to see children disappearing but octogenarians lingering.'

The wimpy grey man supported his head.

Professor Hansel had written copies castigating political parties of failure. He often cried out to the public for a change of mentality in politics. In the course of their discussion, they blamed the S.D.F Chair for dropping the party's decisions and trying to take side with the ruling party. Hansel wasn't of any particular party. All he expected of all political parties was the exercise of fairness in politics, rather than turning it into a dirty game. His dream was for an ideal world. Unfortunately, time was proving him to be an idealist, although his speeches and writings played some role.

The educated crew spoke from one topic to the other, each one sipping some alcohol. They seemed full of wisdom but most of them were broke men.

The deceased's small brother, David Adamu, entered with a tray of champagne flutes. Two minutes later, he entered again with palm wine Indian bamboo tumblers and hopelessly dropped it on the table. He greeted those who just entered.

'More cola nuts please, if you don't mind,' said Hansel. David dashed out. He came back briskly with a plate of more cola nuts.

'God bless you my son,' said a secondary school principal. 'No western markets exist for cola nuts. We won't be chewing these few nuts.'

Hansel pinched some black spots and snapped them away with his fingers. 'We should chew with a second thought,' he said.

'Why not,' another responded. 'If all timber could be on its way to the west, the cola nut tree is no exception.'

'That's right. When the oak, the *iroko*, mahogany, red wood, and other trees disappear, they will soon chase the cola nut tree.'

There was beer, champagne, wine and other soft drinks. Palm wine and corn beer was in a greater quantity.

When David entered the fourth time with more palm wine, the principal looked at him strangely.

'This young man's face seems familiar,' he said. 'Do I know you, boy?'

'I'm David Adamu, Sir.'

'Do you school at C.N.C?'

'I used to.'

'You finished high school…'

'No, Sir. I dropped out a year ago.'

'Why?'

'My parents couldn't meet up. All money was pushed to my late brother's projects but unfortunately…'

David suddenly started weeping. A man felt bad and supported him to a seat. Hansel's look was more depressing. He turned his head and stared at the sky through the window. It was still incredible to Hansel how the times were becoming cruel to the people. It was unbearable. He didn't like the scene.

Some young ladies came in with food. There was pounded coco yams, plantains and koki, and hot pepper soup plantains. Hansel ate a little of the pepper soup and drank some more beer.

He was about to leave and so too some others. He walked, waving goodbye to family members.

'It's the Lord that gives and it's He that takes,' said Hansel to the old couples as he held their hands to raise their spirits. 'Give God a big *thank you* for the death of your son… Take this small amount of money and manage.'

They all went on their knees to thank him. This, they did in tears.

On that day, Hansel had hired a transport bus from an agency that could help take other friends.

It was time for him and friends to leave. The driver was already in the car waiting for the intellectuals. Hansel walked towards the vehicle at the exit of the flower-fenced compound. Tanga followed him for a word.

'Professor,' said Tanga, 'Birget has finally been laid to rest. He was your student. What are your feelings?'

'You don't have to ask me of a feeling. If you do have the details of the story and you're also a human being, then I should feel the way you do. It's more than heartrending.'

'I moved round and many people were so puzzled that the ministry of Higher Education was not represented and no word was sent. Is there any comment or message from you, Sir?'

'It's a perplex thing I can say. The government of this country is making a mockery of its people. Nobody has commented on the death of the deceased. The Ministry of Public Security says the police have the right to quell down any unsolicited uprising. That's great of them but I have this message to the youths. Let us sit together and redefine the factors for these deadly acts. Let us look for the solutions. One of the reasons of these reckless acts by the police is bribery and corruption. If you don't take and do not give bribes, it is the beginning of a better society. It is the beginning of nation reconstruction.'

'What message to the forces of Law and Order?'

'I doubt whether this would reach them or make any meaning. A cracked stone is difficult to close. We had better term them something else. I don't think they were working on the orders from the Ministry. Well, what should one expect from a man who became a police officer without passing the examination. We force them into the profession using corrupt means thinking that we're helping them from crisis. Even people who've never seen the four walls of a classroom have become police officers. Some cannot even spell their names. This is the result- firing at the innocent population. Advising such stark nincompoops is like injecting a death body for recovery. I know there are a few respectable officers amongst them. I do appreciate their efforts but we have many things to do to protect the people on the streets. What do you expect from a man picked from the gutters and handed a gun? This is not the first time, not the second, and not even the tenth... Opening fire on students has become a persistent police culture. Why?

Well, in addition to the thousand epaulettes adorned on their shoulders by the good government, I give them gallantry for good action. They shall live longer than the time God has assigned them not to enjoy but to see the disaster they are causing in our world.'

He jumped into the car followed by other professors.

The bus was soon on traffic leading for Buea. The bus negotiated a corner and from a distance of about one hundred metres, stood three police officers and three gendarmes. One of the police constables raised his right hand and sounded his whistle. Then, the bus slowed. He motioned his right hand, directing the bus to stop ahead, some fifty metres away from them. Just after a side gutter, was a small hut. One of them sat in there. He was like guiding them to do the job.

The officer pocketed his hands with his gun crossed behind, appearing stern. It wasn't any laughing matter.

In a normal day with eighteen passengers, it would be the bus conductor to take car documents to the highway police for checking. This was different. It was a hired bus with an educated crew. The reason the driver had to present the documents himself.

The driver jumped down with some documents. It was an old newspaper well folded. He walked briskly towards the officer and greeted him the way military men would do; His left hand straight down and his right hand rose to above his ears while legs remained straight together.

'Repos,' said the constable in French jokingly. The driver relaxed, extended his hand and greeted him. 'Well done, Chief,' he said with a convincing smile. At the same time, he handed the folded newspaper. Such a style was becoming a police culture.

Meanwhile, the car was idling and the professor and some colleagues watched from the side mirrors. None of the police officers went to the car for control, or to ask passengers for presentation of their national identity cards as was the common practice.

Drivers who would settle the police with five hundred francs were the most loved and most known and were never disturbed once on the highway.

The officer unfolded the newspaper and whipped out some notes. He handed it back unfolded, but his thin face didn't show any satisfaction. He forced a smile but it didn't really show. What was noticed of him was only his thin muscles, red eyes, rough hair, like one malnourished at childhood.

'Do you know this is join control?' he asked. 'One thousand for us and one for the gendarmes is manageable.'

'I'm not on duty. These people hired the bus and paid the money directly to the counter. This small thing is just to lubricate the smooth bond between us, Sir.'

'To maintain a good bond is to add a thousand francs. Don't put me into trouble with my colleagues.'

As they argued, the gendarme sitting in the hut sprang to the policeman. 'This isn't a debate club,' he said. 'Get the keys until he settles his bills.'

The driver heard his car horned. One of the bookmen must have done it.

'Please, I have *Big Men* in the car.'

The constable bubbled in anger walking towards the bus. Perhaps, to make sure those in the car were normal passengers. He saw men, most of them in responsible gorgeous suits. His spirits and the good courage began to fall. He pretended touching the tyres, checking if they were in good condition. Then, he took some steps away from the car and said, 'Laissez le partir. C'est risqué.'

The shouting on the driver quelled and they told him to leave. Hansel had descended to shout at the police but he saw the driver rushing back towards the car. At the same time, a timber truck with three oversize logs of oak wood was approaching. It was at a very high speed. On each log was stamped, *EXPORT*. Hansel jumped over the gutter for safety. Within a second, no one could hear the sound of the truck. It was far gone.

'These are agents working for the vultures that have been swooping over the mountains and going free. You keep molesting innocent chicks that need just a few grains. You should have stopped this truck.' Hansel was directing it to the police officer. 'You should have doubled the amount,' he continued sarcastically, 'to yank yourselves from the agony of hunger. You all look like the intestine of a butterfly. You should keep supporting them in draining all materials. Sooner or later, they'll be exporting human beings like you.'

He thinned his mouth in extreme dissatisfaction shaking his head. The driver chauffeured them off at a respectable speed.

Five

D ays counted fast. It was two weeks since investigations into the death of Williams started. Foti had pushed in more than enough money to pilot the process. The police were to question Grace that evening on her service gun.

At 8 pm that day, four special police investigators stormed Grace's home. Grace Asong was a police officer. She mothered two heady boys and was a widow in a love affair with a businessman, dealing between Cameroon and Dubai. Ngo, the first son was never home. Rene, a second son, sat on a swivel chair with his legs placed on the table. It was his common practice even in the presence of his mother. He stayed there flipping TV channels hopelessly burlesquing like western rappers.

'Good evening,' greeted one of the investigators. 'Is your Mum or Dad in?'

Rene was mute. He also didn't care to look at them to show any concern and pretended as if they were not important.

'Young man, can you talk?' asked another in a grunting voice. 'Is your mother there?'

The young boy motioned his hand pointing to the room but his eyes focused on the screen. It wasn't for any concentration, but for the lone fact of stubbornness. Grace heard them talking.

'Rene, who is there?'

'I don't know,' he responded spitting on the floor. Grace darted and saw four men eagerly standing. 'You this stupid boy,' she abused, 'can't you sit them down?'

'Did I invite them?' Rene fired back. Grace looked at the strange faces. She could feel some strange and cruel thing was in the making.

'Can I help you, Sirs?'

'It will be a pleasure,' responded the eldest calmly, but in an unpredictable way. She offered them seats but was still hugely suspicious.

'We need talk with you in isolation.'

'Why?'

'Please, your son should leave if you don't mind.' She argued further. One of them presented himself as *Member, Special Wing, Buea Criminal Police*. Grace chilled. She was quite aware of this wing and she knew the kind of cases this wing used to handle. She was left with no choice but to respect the orders. Of all police branches in the country, this was the only that gave the citizens the impression that at least not all was bad. They could work just for months and be transferred to other regions. That is the reason they could not be easily identified even by police officers. They had no uniform. It was hard to identify them on the streets. The only doubt by the citizens was the fact that they were not often involved in the daily bad cases.

They were given maximum training such as Public security training, criminology, administration, military, and a high level of sociology and psychology. They were *no laughing matter officers*.

Mula Street was a residential area for first class people, most of them elitists. The interrogation proper started.

'Are you Grace Asong?'

'Yes, Sir.'

'A police officer. Is that right too?'

'Yes, Sir.'

At this moment, a signed questioning warrant was handed to her. She studied it for a few seconds.

'We are probing into the death of one Williams shot dead. Do you know anything about that?'

'Yes.'

'Good. Tell us.'

32

'I'm fan to BAKWA FM. I heard the bad news from that TV channel about two weeks ago.'

'Where were you at the time on the day of the event?'

'I was at home. I am on a month's leave. I am always at home.'

'Thanks very much, Grace.' At this point, the officer relaxed as if all was over. He yawned and the tension in Grace too fell a little. 'Do you have your service pistol with you?'

'Yes, I do.'

'Can we see it if you don't mind?'

'No problem.' Grace fumbled to the bedroom and snatched her handbag. She walked fast back to the sitting room while unzipping it. At first sight, she was taken aback. No pistol. They were seriously watching her in that perplexity. She walked back to her bedroom.

Three minutes passed and she continued searching. It was certain, her pistol wasn't there.

'Please,' one of them said, 'come back if you can't find it.'

She walked back reluctantly, greatly astonished and then sat. 'Can you identify it if presented to you?'

'Yes. Even the serial number of my gun can tell it all.'

At this level, the officers were beginning to understand that it could be out of nonchalance that her pistol wasn't with her. However, they kept on with the interrogation.

'Good,' said the officer taking out a plastic bag with a pistol inside. He handed it to her. She looked at it like magic. It was rightly hers, but she couldn't understand what was going on. This point galled her and raped her of all courage. Incredible indeed!

'How comes?'

'We should be asking you that question... It was found at the scene on the same day.' They looked at her for a couple of minutes, perhaps to extract some guilt. She moved her head from the pistol to the officers every millisecond. She was lost in thoughts.

'Someone must have done this, not me. I left it in my bag and for two weeks now, I haven't checked it. I swear to the Almighty Heavens.'

'Do you suspect anybody?'

'Oh my God!' she exclaimed.

'Why do you call God? Do you suspect Him?'

'Not that. I... I...'

'Say something, lady.'

She was rather dumbstruck, and stressfully coiled her face to grab any scene related to who might have gone with her gun. Her thoughts were just lost.

'No, my sons hardly have access to my room.'

'Who else lives here?'

'My Boyfriend does.'

'Who and where is he?'

'Peterson. He has been in Dubai now for about three weeks and a few days.'

'Where are your two sons? The one outside and...'

'There is another.'

'How are they called?'

'Rene Ndam is out there, and Ngo Ashu.'

'Where is Ngo Ashu?'

'He comes and goes with friends.'

'How old is he?'

'Twenty two years old.'

'When did you lastly see him?'

'A week and a half...'

'Why? Where does he live?'

'He lives with his friends. He doesn't want to stay home.'

'Do you know some of his friends?'

She was quiet for some seconds. Though mute, she was in a fumbling look.

'Can you call your son in if you don't mind?'

She called Rene. He was a stubborn fellow and was never subtle in responses.

'Please, Rene, talk to us. Do you know where Obi lives?'

'Which Obi?'

'The one you said is a friend to Ngo.'

'Are you a policeman? Why terrorise people with too many questions?'

'If I say yes, are you going to respond?'

'Do I owe any responsibility to that?'

Suddenly, a friend to Rene dressed as an American hip-hop super star burlesqued from outside, 'What's up men? Are you ready?'

Rene couldn't listen to the officers any more. 'Hi, nigger,' he responded dashing out. He greeted his friend in an American street boy style and they disappeared. The officers didn't mind.

'I suppose you come with us to the station for more questioning, if you don't mind.'

She panicked a little, looking at the various faces.

'You want to arrest me, isn't it?'

'Well, if you term it *arrest*.'

The officer looked at her. She was stripped of all courage. Astonished, she said, 'So you want to molest me. You want to disgrace me. Am I a suspect?'

'Calm down. Aren't you a police officer? We'll let you enjoy the right of a security officer. However, if you disregard that integrity, we will lend a hand of pain. You see this?' He showed her a pair of handcuffs. 'Now get dressed the way you want.'

Time was running tougher and cruel for Grace. She entered her room bewildered and then yelled. It was only a horse cry. There was no tear when the officers rushed in.

'Yes, come and see my nakedness,' she said placing her dress on her downside. They checked the windows and the protectors were heavy and firm. Thus, she wouldn't escape if left to dress up. They walked back to the sitting room but none of them sat. When she dressed up, she stood there in a painful soliloquy. A situation, just like from sunlight and suddenly into an unannounced heavy down pour. It was quite traumatising. She looked at the spot where her bag used to hang. 'Peterson?' she thought. 'No, it can't be. He left before the incident. Ngo...?'

'Please,' shouted the officer, 'are you ready?'

She walked to them in a mode of no resistance. They were soon in traffic.

Grace had known her son to be of threat but not to the extent of murder. Ngo had fought on the streets, spat on faces, and destroyed properties. That was all she could think of him. It was the gloomiest moment indeed. It was the darkest nightmare than ever before in her life. It wasn't long, she was behind bars.

The following day, the officers set out in various secret groups. They went out searching for Obi and Ngo. More and more information kept coming in. In Buea, Obi's ostentatious room was smashed open after several knocks to no avail.

The police found a new model laptop, two TV sets, a pistol, police uniforms, digital and video cameras, ten kilos of cocaine, two hundred stamps and signatures of administrators on pieces of paper.

A piece of bread pinched by rats for several days found on the table gave them the impression that the occupant of the room had been out for at least a week or two. They snapped the entire room and suspected articles.

It was this same night that another group of special police gathered news that Obi and some friends were on their way to Mamfe. Mamfe was a chief town of the Manyu division in the Southwest region. Mamfe police was informed.

At about four o'clock the following morning, the Buea special wing police officers were advancing with a sure step along the path of motivated justice. The Lord Mayor went extra, turning his pockets just to grease their diligence. From Buea to Mamfe was a distance of about 256km.

Cameroon is a bilingual country of ten regions. Two of them are English speaking- Northwest and Southwest and the two regions border each other.

It was an unfortunate thing that there was no good road linking Buea and Mamfe. The bad boys would always ambush, sometimes even during the day.

They had pictures of Obi and some of his friends to facilitate the search. In addition, they had a current vivid description of Obi and possible friends.

Although they were not really prejudging them, they were ninety-nine percent sure that Obi's group was involved. At about 5 am, they were kilometres towards Mamfe. Heavy petrol tankers and timber trucks had cracked the roads. There was heavy road maintenance and at this point, the road was diverted. Only through a rough stony road of half a mile would a car rejoin the diverted high way. On this rough road, from a distance of about two hundred metres, they saw a car near a corner.

They drove further, this time quite slowly. As they approached and realised that armed robbers had surrendered some men, one of them hurried trying to snatch his pistol. A man darted from behind and shouted, surrendering them. 'If you move, I will shoot.' The officers tried to reverse, but a huge jeep approached from behind. They were now in between the two groups of robbers. They raised their hands surrendering as they saw that the other men too had been surrendered. Two robbers placed their legs on their heads ready to shoot while others searched the car.

'If I get no money, I'll shoot,' said one of them to those on the ground.

'No, Sir, the money is there.'

'Where?'

They couldn't find money. One of them fired up a tree and there was great tremor. The bullets rattled tree branches. There was dead stillness. Only birds chirped frightfully and others squawked, escaping to other trees.

The investigators were asked to lie down. One of them apologised. Just for no crime committed. 'I'm sorry, Sir,' he said.

'You're sorry for yourselves, you embezzlers,' was the response.

'Yes, Sir. Thanks.'

'Now listen to me. We want money. No more, no less. Otherwise, you'll live no more.'

Meanwhile, those searching the car in front found bank notes packed in a spare tyre. The tube had been removed and money packed in it. When they took all money, they asked them to drive fast without looking back. They threw the tyre full of money into their car and joined their colleagues behind to intimidate the investigators.

'Blow heads off, if there's no money,' shouted one of them in serious demonstration of robbery excellence. Their muscles convulsed when they heard this.

'No, Sir, don't kill us. We didn't travel with money.'

'We're not killers,' said the chief robber, 'but snatchers. We snatch our lives from the agony of poverty caused by pregnant men like you.'

'Yes, Sir,' one of them responded in confusion.

'Shut up. Don't *Sir* me you dirty rat. Look at your stomach like an inflated balloon. From where do you get money to blow this thing big?'

When he said so, he raised his foot to the investigator's head. Others were searching seriously in the car. The spare tyre was knifed open, but nothing found. One of the robbers venomously tore off one of the investigator's chest pockets and snatched his wallet. He opened it. In it was a card like an identity card, written on it *Special Wing, Criminal Police Inspector, Buea*.

'Criminal Police!' exclaimed the robber.

'No, Sir. Yes, Sir,' fumbled one of the police investigators.

'Now, you're investigating. Is that correct?'

No one spoke a word. All were gripped in terror.

'You don't want to talk. Alright, tell us who you're investigating and why you want to do so.'

Still, all were mute and in serious angst.

'Tell us who has ever interrogated you for taking bribes... Now I've taken your names and if next time you don't pay your taxes to us for having these big stomachs, it shall cost you your lives. Is that right?'

'Yes, Sir,' they all answered in anguished voices.

'Come on! Get up and drive off without looking back.'

In seconds, they jumped into the car and only squeal of the wheels was heard as it gradually faded off.

No matter all odds, they still reached Mamfe.

* * * *

Betrayal and intrigues was a common practice. It existed amongst all class of persons- the poor and rich. It existed amongst people of this world and those of the other world.

The story was that a friend of Obi had been thrown out of the group for being two faced when interrogated on a deal that had leaked out. In that deal, the friend had been on a higher risk but received a lesser amount of money.

The friend that had been thrown out thought that his hand that triggered, effacing the life of a lawyer should have earned him half the amount that was paid to that group. When Obi acted as a Chief Don, under estimating his importance and giving him a smaller share of the money, he leaked the secret killing of that legal face.

Still, the big Dons that had paid for the execution of that heavy murder had bought the minds of all detectives assigned for that investigation.

This friend had directed the investigators. It was for this reason that they were sure to dismantle the Obi group.

* * * *

Before they got to Mamfe, ten policemen and five gendarmes commenced the investigations. The investigators joined them.

In Mamfe, there was a small town called Tinto. There was a story that two years back, a Tinto politician had been murdered for being too radical in public. His wife died abroad as a refugee. The deceased's only son, Tabi Eric was at this time the only occupant. Tabi had been repatriated from Germany just when his mother died there.

Things had never been favourable for Tabi. The Cameroon police, when handed by the German police had detained him for six months.

Tabi had always believed that he was born with an obscured destiny. It was the reason he wanted to do anything. 'If I am not of this world, I should be of the underworld,' Tabi had said. He became a member of the Obi group due to this pessimism in life. The house he inherited from his parents was now used often by the robbers.

* * * *

They had just entered at four that morning. The compound was fenced. Outside and along the fence were hibiscus flowers. At this time, the gate was keyed.

At cockcrow, the police officers and gendarmes surrounded Tabi's residence. They all hid themselves behind the flowers, and they were on the brink of something they would know soon. They could perceive some kind of smell

40

like bad sent from some poisonous plants. At other moments, it was like toxic smell from burnt dresses.

They were scared but ready. There was a bell at the gate and a red light spot on it. One of the gendarmes went to it, rang it, and listened. For about two minutes, no word came and no one moved. A few minutes later, they heard a cracked voice asked, 'What a beast at that gate?'

The security officers all adjusted. At this point, they were confident to trap them. First cocks continue to crow. They heard a man walking and whistling on a small path just a few metres away from them. One of the officers tiptoed to him. 'Shp,' he hissed. 'Don't move. If you do, I shoot.' It was a young truck pusher on his way for his daily bread. He immediately went down on his knees and raised his hands submissively.

'Do you live here?'

'Yes, Sir. Don't kill me please.'

'I am not out for you. Do you know who lives here?'

'Yes. Tabi, Sir.'

The bad boys could feel that things were not in order. From inside, Tabi shifted the window blind. He studied the environment for some time, and noticed flowers shaking strangely. It wasn't long when the security officers heard a heavy gun bombed three times from inside. They fired back ten times in response, all directed into the air. The vibration of the sound could determine how ready the officers were. It also made them know what kind of weapons they had with them. They were ready to smash the gate.

The young man on his knees could now understand what was going on.

'Please,' the truck pusher said pointing to a small hole leading to a gutter, 'he'll escape there.'

'Are you sure?'

'Yes, Sir. He has dug a tunnel from his house to that place there. There is an outlet there.'

The officer, without any doubt and waste of time motioned his fingers for three other officers to come. He asked the rest to break the gate. Three gunshots scattered the gate lock and they smashed the gorgeous gate open. Then, like military men, they forced the main door open and immediately retreated to the sides of the door expecting a counter attack. No one came for them. They swooped in, pointing their guns from one corner to the other.

Out of the house, like a rat mole, a robber sprang from an outlet into the gutter. Two gunshots immediately came from two of the officers. He was shot on the arm and leg. His gun fell. They closed his mouth and tugged him to the side. As they continued to wait, death began to smell. Officers inside the house opened fire at the least dark corner of the house. They switched on all lights. Inside a room like a small temple, they found a gun still very warm. The owner had just dropped it there. It smelled as if the owner had just fired it.

There was a small carpet of about two metres square on the floor. It seemed it had just been turned. They moved it a little and found a square line cut into the floor. That was the cover and gateway into the tunnel where they had escaped. They pulled the small cement board off. The inside of the hole was dark. The bandits were inside creeping to escape. They were like trapped animals.

A sharp sound came. Someone was in pains in the tunnel. They could feel the danger at the exit of the tunnel as they could see blinking shadows. Still, they were sneaking.

An officer fired into the tunnel from inside the house. They fumbled towards the outlet. All were panting terribly. Still, they crawled forward with pistols ready to shoot at the least obstruction.

Tabi was intelligent and smart in action. Just two metres to spring out from the tunnel, he took a breath and listened. He pulled off his T-shirt and threw it to the left to displace attention. Then he immediately sprang to the right.

At first sight of the T-shirt, an officer fired several times. Though Tabi was about a few metres gone, it was unfortunate. They shot him at the ankle and he fell gasping. One officer rushed, handcuffed him and left him at the spot.

One after the other, as they were jumping out from the tunnel, they were all arrested.

Soon to be breaking news was: Armed Robbers Arrested in Mamfe, or, Murderers of the Mayor's Son Arrest.

Six

There was tension everywhere. There was tension both in radio and newspaper houses.

Who could be the next, just like Williams? Many people doubted whether the alleged criminals would be convicted and sentenced for killing Williams. Indeed, it was going to be a case that even those who hated the courts would like to witness.

For about a week, Grace Asong was behind bars and sick too. She was getting slacker every second. The officers kept interrogating her expecting some revelations but she declined all responsibilities saying she couldn't explain who took her pistol.

To many people, it was incredible that her service gun was involved in the case. She was in some parched soliloquy that was draining her of all courage. There were legal jargons such as *Accomplice, Accessory, Felony, Capital Murder, Firing squad* and others. Legal jokers were waiting and rehearsing such words.

Tanga had reported, 'Murderers of the mayor's son have been arrested by forces of law and order in Mamfe...'

It wasn't long before counsels for the defendants referred to the report as, 'Prejudged Report.' They said, 'Only when our clients are proven guilty, can they be termed murderers.'

Lawyers were after Tanga, pressurising him to withdraw the word *murderers* and to use *alleged criminals*. Motions had been filled in Court for their release on bail, but the judge had turned them all down.

'Counsels need respect ethics of this noble profession. This is a case competent before the military tribunal. Even if pushed to be heard by this court, this is a felony and not a simple offence, nor a misdemeanour. This motion can't work. The defendants must remain in custody until hearing.'

Those were the words of the judge and he stood by it.

That same week, a new press law was out. It gave the right to private radio stations to report on certain political issues only after the government radio station must have covered it. In violation of the decree, such a station would be issued an injunction.

* * * *

The atmosphere was tense and fierce. It was becoming more dangerous to walk in the night. The Head of State had promised his people, 'This shall be a government of action. It shall be a government of enjoyment and the privileges man could afford to think will reach every individual. The dividends of this democracy shall be distributed evenly. I'm carrying freedom to every household and right to every individual, big or small. There shall be freedom of expression in all forms. We shall speak the language of the poor, the lame, the blind... I mean we shall speak love and the respect for all.'

Those were the sweet words at the birth of democracy and multi-party system. People had been expecting those words to yank humanity from the agony and sorrows inflicted by foreign masters and to drive the entire nation into a promising 21st century. Yet, some said it was becoming worst than a devastating storm. The head of state had not visited Tiko or the entire region for long. To Professor Hansel and others, 'It's one of the greatest nonchalance of a thing. It's the highest neglect.'

Again, Hansel had cried, 'No, the 21st century has come with a serious downpour that is now penetrating the cracked walls. Only the fern and moss plant have been growing on the walls. Both our ruling and rival parties have failed.'

What he meant, many people couldn't give any interpretation. The only understanding was that the Head of the country had been named premier of the country for several years and later in 1982 was named the overall head.

From one party system that was abolished in 1990, into multiparty and then into the early hours of the 21st century, he had still to consolidate his political stance. Until then he was never wrong as many people criticised.

On the other side, the National Chairman for SDF had addressed many issues for over a decade since the birth of democracy. Nevertheless, all efforts had shoved militants into worst woes. The party leaders had failed and were still failing to agree amongst themselves. The result was that it divided into factions, thereby weakening its strength. A journalist editorialised his report, 'I find no reason to support SDF to take power because they blame CPDM for all ills, but still, they do same ills and even more. I know one SDF militant who has more than thirty billions in his account but is unable to establish just a small firm so as to employ a few people, but has that audacity to condemn the ruling party for not creating jobs. From top to bottom, they are corrupt people that want to dance the same old dance.'

Many demonstrations by the SDF had called the attention of some international organisations to assess actions by the CPDM.

There was rumour that the chairman for the SDF would take residence at the national capital than remain where the party was born and which was its strongest hold. Militants were accusing the party whips for having accepted the party chair taking residence at the national capital.

Feh had defended himself on many occasions.

It was Sunday and would soon dawn Monday. It was the day Obi and friends would appear before the judge in a military tribunal. It would be a travesty of justice due to the fact that such murder cases had become rampant. That is the reason the matter would be thrashed out in Buea in an extraordinary way.

Seven

The court was ready to hear from the alleged criminals. It was March. The mayor and his entire family were still behind, but the court was already jamb to full capacity. Many prominent members of the opposition parties were present in court. Before the mayor's arrival, examination of the defendants had begun.

During preliminary investigations, the accused persons had admitted that they killed the victim but said nothing of the reason d'être. Thus, convicting them wasn't any big deal. The people were eager to know the reason for such a dramatic tragedy.

The mayor entered the courtroom bent with humble steps as a sort of respect for the state. The defendants occupied the first bench as if they were actors watched by the audience and the legal personnel in mumbling debates. Mayor Foti had not recognised Obi when he entered the courtroom. The police had deformed Obi's face. Bandages covered his forehead.

'Now,' continued the judge, 'Obi, tell us why you people decided to kill him.'

At this time, Foti blinked several times, stretching his head forward when he heard the name *Obi*. Still, he was not convinced.

'Speak, Obi,' continued the Judge. 'You're the eldest in this group… Why did you decide to kill him?'

'I didn't kill him,' said Obi. 'Ngo did.'

The mayor was moved. He was convinced that it was the Obi he had contracted with to kill Tanga. The mayor's body convulsed. As Obi talked, he turned his head to look at the mayor. There was a lot of concern. The court was in a fumbling watch. The Judge looked at them in confusion.

'Ngo, why did you decide to gun Williams? You did, right?'

'It was a mistake…'

'Mistake?' asked the Judge with more concern.

Ngo, appearing wimpy, was silent. Rather, he turned his head and looked at his mother, a co-defendant. Her charge was that she was an accessory to the crime. On her part, Grace looked at her son and her tears refreshed.

'Did you say mistake?'

'Yes, Sir.'

'What do you mean? Explain to the court.'

'We thought it was Tanga. Obi cued me. Then, I did shoot. I am so sorry, Sir.'

Tanga was present in court that day. He had been jotting on a paper in his file. When he heard his name, he suddenly stopped breathing. The file dropped from his hands and his mouth went ajar.

The Judge smartly jotted a few points down and asked again.

'Who is Tanga?' he asked with his ears up this time.

'He is a journalist, Sir.'

'Do you know him?'

'Yes, Sir.'

'Do you know him in person?'

'Yes, Sir.'

Foti collapsed at the right side of the hall. The scene suddenly turned baffling as the Judge ordered that they rush him to the hospital. The police scrambled to give him assistance and the court was in a buzz of voices but the clerk shouted for order. Tanga chilled. He leaned on the wall chained in thoughts. Indeed, it was a starkly and dreading revelations.

He was well known and his presence anywhere was never obscured. The Judge caught eyes with Tanga, and his pen tapping on his beard. Over the frame of his glasses, he still kept looking at him.

'Please, Sir,' said the Judge to Tanga, 'can you come forward if you don't mind?'

He never spoke a word but walked to the front. This time, his eyes focused on the murderers.

'Ngo, do you know this man?'

'Yes, Sir, it is the man I was asked to fire at.'

'Who asked you to fire?'

'Obi whistled and I did it.'

'Why did he ask you to shoot?'

'I don't know.'

At this level, he kept quiet. His eyes focused on his toes. The judge shouted at him.

'If you don't want to talk, you will go to prison. You just wanted to kill him without a single reason?'

'Yes, Sir. I was just to fire at him and get my share of the money.'

'Share of money from where?'

'From Obi.'

'… Your mother gives you money and so too her boyfriend. Why did you do the mess?' asked the judge casually and rhetorically as he was making some jottings.

Ngo was quiet. For several minutes, the Judge questioned them to dig out if there was something or someone who engineered the killing. They were all silent, even after all sorts of threats from the judge. All that was lucid was the confession.

The process had been smooth tongued. The only obscurity was why they killed him and why the mayor collapsed. Perhaps, some thought, because his son was mistakenly shot.

The court session was over. The court was to sit again the following week. It was clear, except otherwise, capital punishment was in the offing for the defendants. There was premeditation, they used lethal weapons, they committed the act and murder was complete. They were in clear senses. They were mentally sound at the time of the act. These were the ingredients the lawyers for defendants couldn't keep aside so as to win the case for their clients.

There were no arguments to put as a defence for them. Moreover, the most important, they claimed responsibility.

Just in front of the court, there were some buzzes. Some people knew the hatred people had for Tanga and how the mayor had plotted on several occasions to defame him. Thus, they suspected the mayor in the complicated incident.

* * * *

At the Hospital, as nurses were resuscitating Foti, his son Kennedy rushed in with words about some rumours. When he entered, the nurses were out. Kennedy's mother sat just besides the bed. 'Dad, are you alright?' asked Kennedy.

'Yes, my son.'

'Sure? Can you walk?'

'Yeah.'

'Let him rest,' said Abiga. 'The doctor said he needs rest. There is nothing too serious.'

For some minutes, Kennedy lingered in front of the private ward expecting some minutes to pass so he could talk with his father.

Nurses and other medical personnel were moving up and down hospital corridors, some pushing corpses on stretchers.

Kennedy was lost in thoughts. He soon realized himself and rushed in. This time, his father managed to sit.

'Dad, is it alright?'

'Yes, Ken. Don't worry much. It shall be well.'

'I should, Dad,' responded Kennedy frowning. There was a knock at the door. It was Kingsley. If there would be any scandal, he would be seriously involved, for they were political lovebirds. From Kingsley's face, there was an expression of some secret overtures.

He kept cool when he entered. His low spirit provoked fear in the mayor's heart.

'Any problem, King?' asked the mayor.

'Yes, but not serious. We'll talk it out later.'

Kennedy couldn't hold his tongue. He knew how intimate his father had been with Kingsley. On his part, Kingsley was scared to talk it out in the presence of Kennedy and Abiga.

'Dad,' said Kennedy, 'there is a big scandal out there.'

'What is it?'

'The accused persons said they were hunting for Tanga but mistakenly shot at my brother and there is a rumour that you are involved.'

'Yes,' Kingsley confirmed and continued, 'and the matter has been fixed for another hearing for reasons of more investigations as to why they wanted to kill Tanga.'

Foti was swept away. Beyond all doubts, he raised his head with both palms, appearing accountable. For some time, he remained quiet and lost.

'When is the court sitting next?' he asked.

'In a week,' said Kennedy and Kingsley in chorus.

His wife was dumbstruck. She knew her husband could be involved in such deals but never thought or knew that their son's death was supposed to be for Tanga.

He pushed aside the blanket with his legs and climbed down the bed in uncertainty. His wife held him to sit.

'Where are you going?' she asked.

'Didn't you hear the scandal? Do you want them to efface my political stance?'

'And what do you want to do about it?'

He was quiet. Rather, he looked wildly at Kingsley as if he wanted him to say a word. Yet, both of them only held eyes in bewilderment.

'Dad,' said Kennedy, 'you have to meet the Judge and his people at the hotel to put things in order.'

'Kingsley, what do you think?'

'Yes, Ken is right. We need to meet the Judge for arrangements if possible.'

It would be politically ruinous and legally cataclysmic if things were not done faster.

The Judge was a French speaking Cameroonian. He appeared too tough on his face. Over the years, the mayor had the experience that such a hash face could be made brittle by proposing huge sums.

The judge would need to communicate with counsels in case he would want to divert the case.

Information about the scandal seemed to have cured Foti. He insisted to the doctors that he was in good condition and wanted to retire home.

That day was gone and it dawned to another.

* * * *

The following day, the National Chair for the opposition party was to address issues on political success of the party, reaching the farmers, HIV and AIDS, briefings on the 2011 election and on the reasons why he decided to take residence at the national capital, Yaoundé.

The occasion was about to begin at the Tiko central. Present at the occasion were party militants, Member of Parliament for the area, former deputy mayor, parliamentary leader, and the general secretary for the party, party scouts, councillors and many others.

There were songs after songs from a musical set. There were songs of freedom of expression. There were also songs of democracy. Ward chairpersons were with various groups under huts.

In addition, there were several dance groups from various tribes ready to tell the party leaders how much they expected from a democratic Cameroon.

The Party's spokesperson stood with a microphone reading out the agenda. The chairperson sat and the secretary was on his right and the parliamentary chairperson on his left. They all sat on an elevation watching the desperate faces holding pieces of paper with various writings, *Let my people go, SDF must rule, Nde Feh is our president, Party in power must quit. We need change.*

Life was so incomprehensive. There was misery. Hunger was approaching. Due to global warming, crops like coco yams and rice wasn't doing well any longer. That horrible situation made things too bad.

At this occasion, traditional heads were absent. At the birth of democracy, many of them took side with the ruling party and they were declared an auxiliary of the administration. It obliged them to be sympathisers of the ruling party or lose their posts.

Mr. Feh had talked for several minutes. There was rowdy applause.

He came to the point of addressing the issue of accepting the offer to reside at the national capital. His voice suddenly lowered.

'Well, I have received hundreds of letters on that. Some were open letters. Some others were with hidden identities.'

He paused for several seconds. His lips thinned. He was two faced. His right hand rose to his mouth as he cleared his throat and gulped.

'Taking residence at the capital city was a smooth tongued idea of all parties. It wasn't an SDF idea. A budget was debated upon and a law was passed. Giving in for that idea doesn't mean taking side with the ruling party but it is emancipation of our financial strength and location.

This is a fight we have waded waist deep. We have lost souls. It's slow but I hope it is steady and gradually shooting towards a triumphant stage. It might be difficult now to give a practical definition to the word *democracy* because it goes alongside with words as *rights* and *freedom* which are rare. But rest assured that we are up there fighting for you to enjoy the privileges due democracy. We have gone all this far. We are still all that far but we have to be there…'

At this time, there was a feeble applause. He shook his head courageously and smiled.

'SDF,' he enchanted and the people responded, 'power.'

'SDF.'

'Democracy.'

'SDF.'

'Development.'

'SDF.'

'Freedom.'

Drums beat and trumpets and whistles tore the air and then suddenly faded.

'Thousands of people have died since the struggle for a multiparty system. Lethal weapons have been used to abuse the people. Grenades, guns, water cannons, tea gas, are all the bad weapons we can all name. You can see some of our people who have become amputees. Should we give up the struggle at this stage and suffer from the weight of dictatorship just for the reason of the chairman taking residence at the nation's capital?

Youths, rise now and don't dream away your future. Let us join in same accord and say no to killings of students and the assassination of political leaders and journalists. Let's join together and protect our forest that is on the drain to the west. Say no to our petrol sold cheaper in Europe than back home. Say no to our money being dumped in western banks by individual politicians. Say no to high taxes, corruption. We have no study facilities in this country. That is why our children study abroad and after studies, they are assimilated by the west. The illiterate or unsuccessful ones are deported and while at our airports, they are often detained by the police. Most often, they have to give a bribe before release. We are saying no to that practice and that is why I want to be president of this blessed country. There are a group of most important people that are forgotten in this country. This, I mean the farmers. They will be the first people on the agenda of my administration if I become president…'

His entourage rose in roof-splitting applause. The audience was enchanted and equally rose. It was a great emancipation for the chairperson.

He slowed his speech and in a more lubricated voice said, 'I hope I have spoken to an understanding… Even in the midst of the bullet, we shall preach the gospel to the thirsty people. Even with a ban on public rallies, we will preach the gospel on treetops. Even in the pool of blood oozing from the bodies of our murdered youths, we'll still preach the gospel. Let support come from the west to them, we'll still win the battle, come 2011 elections. Let them keep detonating their lethal weapons. We stand fearlessly to win the hand of justice in peaceful demonstration, as our resistance shall destroy those barriers. We are a people that hate war… We are a winning people.'

Those words tore the surroundings, raising all to their feet in thunderous handclapping and shouting.

A needy man is easily convinced. A hungry and desperate man can gulp before thinking that he should have chewed.

The parliamentary chair heaved and rose. He had extreme features- a large stomach, considerable height… He was dressed in an extra ordinary studded gown. He rehearsed the party's popular slogan three times with his right hand raised as sign of strength and emancipation.

'In the midst of intimidation from the ruling and undesirable party, we shall proceed. In the midst of the killing of students by reckless policemen, we shall, and must proceed. Let the blood of Bergit flow to paint the wall of justice. Let also the blood of Bot Kamso pour like rain to drain the assassins. Let your tears in sun in dry seasons and in rain in rainy seasons only go to grease the path to justice. Let our cries compose triumphant songs of integrity. My dear people, permit me quote Martin Luther, *unearned suffering is redemptive…*'

The articulate man couldn't continue. Onlookers were supper excited and their drums deafened all ears. Some dance group leaders passed forward, waiving tassels made from animal skins and painted with the colours of the SDF flag. They danced and walked to the parliamentarian, waved handkerchiefs, and turned back to their seats.

'We're starting our real campaigns soon,' he continued. 'We have passed through hell for several years, during campaigns and on election days. We are facing molestation but we still stand for the truth. We shall not retreat nor shall we surrender. We shall not retaliate to their ardent brutality. But we shall peacefully walk forward in the spirit of fair play, trust, and the respect for humanity. We have just investigated that fake national identity cards have been issued to both mature and under aged people to vote for them. Don't get moved by that. That is to testify that they are fighting a lost battle.'

It was getting to 6 pm and the population began to disperse.

* * * *

Tanga had become a real TV celebrity. Events of arrest, threats, and controversies drove him to be so diligent to his journalistic convictions. It was for this reason that both national and international eyes were on him. It reached a stage where international stations would link him up for a report. He was versed with Cameroon politics and that of neighbouring countries, the reason for which *News International,* with courtesy of BAKWA FM always had him reporting from Cameroon on the Cameroon- Nigerian mineral war.

Tanga had decided to always board a bus since the murder incident. He feared his car being identified and possible attacks. He would leave for Buea every night to hide himself there. There was a big bus stop just half a kilometre from the Tiko central town. Tiko road was a single lane type. Cars from opposite directions would slow down, while bypassing each other. The bus park was for Sure Travel Agency, one hundred metres from the main road.

Tanga stood at the roadside. He had already secured a seat for himself and was waiting for kick-off.

There was a timber truck coming from a distance with three oversize logs of wood. On each log was stamped *FRANCE*. It meant the wood was to be exported to France. The truck was at the speed of about a hundred and twenty kilometres per hour.

A BMW car approached from the opposite direction. It gradually slowed as the truck approached at top speed. Part of the road was covered with thick grass. The road at this point was in C form. There was no clear visibility for any approaching driver.

With great recklessness, the truck rushed and climbed, passing over on the BMW. Tanga stamped his hands on his face, shouting, 'God!'

People swooped towards the squeezed car. They saw what human eyes could not recognise.

Gendarmes and police were immediately informed. They arrived at the scene thirty minutes later and hacked the car. Headless corpses were studded in the crushed BMW. Mangled corpses! It was seriously terrible. Nothing at all was recognised as the car and the intellectuals were reduced to rubbles. All five people in the car were dead! Really, it was a horrific scene.

In that pool of blood, none of them, even from what they wore, was recognised. The desperate population yelled with hands on their jaws eagerly waiting to know names of the crushed.

However, the police officers managed to take out the headless corpses and placed them at the roadsides. Papers and national identity cards coloured with blood were taken from each pocket and the blood wiped. The names were written on a paper and read to the watching population.

Bad news! Amongst them was a most popular writer and professor, Benson. Two others were associate professors, one BAKWA FM journalist and a professional driver. They were all history at this time of the day.

Professor Benson had just published his fifth novel and was on his way for a meeting in preparation for its launching. Unfortunately, he would never see the public consume the beautiful craft he had just designed.

When the police pronounced the words, 'A journalist, Bindeh,' Tanga's body convulsed and he cried, 'God! Why... No. Not Bindeh.' Those words couldn't move Bindeh from his permanent rest. He was gone.

The whole town packed full at the sorrowful and unbelievable, though, real scene. The damage was real. Nothing was going to reverse the act. There was no need for any doctor to confirm. There was no magic for a human head to be joined back to its body.

That particular road was too narrow for such important commercial activities. It was an important road used for general transport and for the transportation of petrol. Yet, no one seemed to care about it. The most important was the export of timber and oil. Therefore, they deliberately allowed the road to bury the torchbearers and openers of a closed society.

It was because of Bindeh and other veterans that BAKWA FM and other private stations were banned several times. Bindeh was known for his popular Saturday one hour show, *Reaching The Politicians*. On the program, he would question politicians, great men, on how they accomplished their successes and how the future would look. His arrest had come twice when he questioned the electoral commission, but he was released on the two occasions following appeals from both national and international human rights organisations.

Tanga couldn't continue his journey as planned. He followed the police and gendarmes to the Tiko mortuary where the corpses were dumped. The police made their report but allowed the truck driver to continue his journey with reasons that the goods were for export.

A town that just listened to its dream leader deliver a word of hope, suddenly subdued to sorrows. Nobody knew when his own time would come, but there was a feeling that anything could happen at any time. It could be in the nearest future or some other time. Unfortunately, it would always be something horrific. It could be a police detonation. It could be the beautiful men of the underworld. It could be a grip by the synthetic viruses. Better still, it could be from the tortures of economic dilemma.

Later on that night, Tanga himself at the anchor of the BAKWA FM radio made the announcements. 'Late night obituary page,' he cried abnormally and then paused. 'Death again! Death has plucked off the ripest fruits….' He choked but tried to continue. 'Eloquent professor and also a veteran of this house… are no more. Mighty Heavens stretch thy hand and help thy creation!' Tanga further cried.

A scary, desperate, useless and hair-raising night…. Even those not related to the deceased persons hated themselves.

Suddenly, Tanga lost control of the announcements. His feeble and sorrowful words sank into the ears of listeners. A collaborator with him at the technical control panel interjected pathetically, 'T2,' as Tanga was often called by his colleagues, 'be strong. Be a man.'

Early the following day, the shocking and ugly news hit the entire nation. Benson was an English speaking professor often suppressed by other professors due to his hash and aggressive writings, though he was well known for his incomparable lectures. He had been relegated of duties as vice chancellor to a simple professor. He was once suspended when he accompanied professor Hansel to a political preaching and launched an attack on most politicians of the ruling party for being passive on both national and international affairs. It was for this reason that he abstained from political occasions.

The chair for SDF, professors, journalists and others still packed the accident scene the following morning.

'This is a challenge and at the same time an embarrassment to the human race,' said professor Hansel. Tanga was there too, wimpy and appearing too hopeless. He was completely lost in thoughts. For a long time, no one heard him talk.

Why only the icons? Many people asked that question. Perhaps gorgeous things are easily seen, was the answer some of them gave.

* * * *

Both the ruling and opposition parties never moved Hansel to favour any of them completely. That was the dream of all the parties. He was intelligent and could draw a big population wherever he went. Many proposals had been made for him to join the administration but he had always turned them down. The most important thing he always lectured on, on public occasions was the respect for human integrity. Some critics described him as a sceptic. Some others described him as a politically low-spirited man. Others called him a political sphinx.

Nevertheless, the award winning professor was a man of adequate and recommended diction. He loved equality amongst all people. He loved words. He loved speaking with his pen, computer and sometimes, making pieces of paper on his table his pillow.

Hansel wasn't good at tables. It was not because he lacked manners but because of the lone fact that he was addicted to books. Indeed, Hansel was a book junky. Some days, early in the morning, he would sip once from his coffee cup and immediately move to his bookshelf. He would discover his coffee only after about half an hour already cold. Sometimes, he would push the saucer aside with his eyes focused on a particular page of a book.

He loved lectures on political morals and etiquettes on all professions. To him, if trading on African leaders' consciences by the western world could stop, Africa would triple on economic growth just within a year.

Eight

Weeks later, in the start of April, people were ready to listen to the judge deliver judgement in the murder case of Williams. They also expected the deceased to be buried after the same judgment. The mayor's two daughters were still in the States. The matter, as the mayor thought, was severe. Thus, he didn't want his daughters to come home.

They were mourning daily by phone. Close friends couldn't understand why they didn't come home when their brother died. Family members thought the girls were westernised, but the truth was just that the mayor feared attack on his daughters.

Though the day was bright, the mayor had big stress. Whether the judge was to sentence the criminals to death by firing, wasn't going to reverse the death of Williams. 'If he was never satisfied with the sum, you've got to watch out,' said Commissioner Kingsley as they were to leave for court that early morning.

'I think he was satisfied,' said Foti in response. 'We are not still at that level.'

'What is the level then?'

'We have become business friends. He has promised to connect Kennedy to the minister of education for contracts to construct some buildings.'

'Good.'

'But that's not important. I would like Kennedy to leave the country.'

'Is that?'

'Yes. I don't want to miss him like Williams. I think it's a little bit safer over there.'

'What about your daughters? Aren't they coming home?'

'No. I have many political rivals both within and without the party. My family is a target…'

He suddenly paused and reflected. Many events seemed to have echoed in his mind. He shook his head like someone in the midst of thought torture. Then he yawned. 'But you know those within this party that want to kick me out.'

'Yes,' the Commissioner replied, 'that's our politics. What do you expect? If you could kick out, then you too could be kicked out.'

Fairness was rare. There was no justice felt. However, it's like the people were getting accustomed with such a prevailing situation. Professor Hansel in one of his political pieces condemned any political move not backed by the word *justice*.

'Let politics be defined as he who gains what, and how, in a struggle for power, or the seizure, consolidation and control of power. If any political undertaking goes without the application of justice and respect for human integrity in all aspects, it is a colossal abuse of power.'

Further, he explained, 'To say there is good governance, the same people who chose the leaders should and must, according to the laws in place, enjoy the privileges… and at the same time have the full right to change their minds if the party in power proves not to meet up the task it stands for. That is what I understand to be true democracy and freedom.'

In some other writings, Hansel condemned African political systems and their leaders for dishing the dividends of democracy only to those who protect their stay in power.

To him, 'any political action not felt by a common needy man, whether he supports them or not, but only by the administrators, is an exploitative step and an abuse of the human ego.'

Thus, people like the mayor, for sure, would hate people like Hansel because his approach to politics seemed different.

* * * *

Before their arrival in court, many people had taken seats expecting the judgment they thought would be calamitous to the criminals. The population was twice the previous hearing. Perchance, there were high speculations that the judgment would be damaging.

There was great tension. There was no doubt because the defendants never declined responsibilities. The serial number of the gun was documentary evidence which was enough proof that Grace Asong's hand was seriously involved. It was unfortunate that she didn't consult a lawyer for her case.

For a longer time, the judge's eyes were over the frame of his glasses and his head bent.

'You say your mother never gave you the gun, is that correct?' asked the judge.

'No, sir,' Ngo answered in a feeble voice.

'Did your mother hear of the murder after the act?'

Ngo was silent. The other defendants had refused responding to questions.

'Ngo, you don't want to answer more questions,' continued the judge. 'Now that you have admitted that you killed Williams, what do you think we can do to you? Tell the court. Say it yourself.'

Still, there was no answer. The judge shook his head in disappointment and said, 'Other laws would get you hanged. Our penal law says you be shot dead. Are you alright?' Ngo was still silent.

These kinds of questions were rare. When the audience heard the judge asking, there was astonishment.

Ngo shivered. He turned his head to the other criminals and back to same position. Grace looked at her son with collapsing eyes, squeezing them, and then tears started flowing.

'Ngo,' she cried. 'You've killed me!'

The Judge delivered the judgment. They were all to face a firing squad. Grace Asong was to face two years imprisonment with a fine of seven million francs CFA. From preliminary investigations, it was proven that she knew her son was involved in the killing but raised no alarm.

The judgement didn't carry the names of Tanga and the mayor. The mayor had fought hard to shape the judgment. The defendants had confirmed they were aiming at Tanga. Yet, it ended there.

* * * *

Delivering a firing squad sentence was one thing but the modus operandi was the greatest doubt. Such a sentence could only be executed after the signature of the President of the republic.

Possibly the judgment would add the number of unexecuted files on shelves in most of the courts. The president had never signed such a file. There were doubts and criticisms. Sentencing such guilty criminals like the defendants during the time of the former Head of state was by hanging. The law on the issue was amended. This time, came the firing squad. Many writings had questioned the disappearance of prisoners from detention camps and the lingering of others without charges.

The condemned criminals were handcuffed and taken away, awaiting execution. Some alleged criminals were in same detention camp for more than three years. The big question was what would be the compensation for someone sentenced to two years in prison, but who had been in detention for three years during long investigations.

Most of such questions had never received any answers. It was well known that the delivering of judgment would be faced with two laws: The written existing law and the law he would feel and pass in benefit of doubt or as well twist it in the name of judicial precedence. Most at times, such judges were considered infallible. Central Prison registered hundreds of deaths and escapes.

A professor once described the conditions of the prisoners there as the *commands of Satan*: scabies, malnutrition, HIV and AIDS, diarrhoea, bed bugs, jiggers, and many other unknown illnesses.

Another writer described them as the living corpses in prison.

* * * *

A week was gone and the mayor's son was laid to rest. Things were in a collapse within the Tiko local government. Councillors began accusing the mayor for many irregularities. Local Newspapers carried headlines such as, *Unexecuted Contracts, Contracts Awarded to Sons, A Man suspected to Have Tasted His Own Cooked Soup, Large Sums Dumped in Western Banks.*

In that same period, there were threats from the Governor of the region to suspend BANKWA FM for reporting on issues that concerned the lives of individual Politicians and the Ruling Party.

Nine

He wasn't only good in constructing words for the public. Tanga was always well dressed. Most often, he was always in a sober suit, a hat, and in Italian square headed shoes. Always with a briefcase, he appeared gentle, calm and soft spoken.

A man supposed to be neutral according to the ethics of his profession, was pushed to take sides.

For that reason, the mayor, after his son's burial, planned a second time to kill Tanga. Kennedy, his other son, and his friend, Kingsley wished to help him execute this cruel plan.

That evening at the mayor's residence was Kingsley, the mayor's wife, Kennedy, and the mayor himself.

'There is only one option now,' said Foti.

'You mean…'

'We need to kill him and burry the corpse ourselves. That is the plan. No one can tell whether I risk losing my son again. Who knows whether I am the next person?'

For some few minutes, he was quiet and then he said, 'Don't feel sad for him. You can see he has raped my political brain and has painted me as murderer, dictator and…'

'You are going too far, higher than the sky,' interrupted his wife. 'Better we stop this stuff. It's a dirty game.'

'Stop what?' asked Foti with an authoritative look. His wife was of the idea that he better surrender politics so that they could meet their daughters in the States. He warned her giving the reason that life in the states was hard and that it would be better for them to leave the country only when they must have gathered more than enough money.

For all this while, Kingsley had just been listening. He sipped again from his glass and said, 'As I know, if you are not a young hustler with enough energy in the States, life becomes hard. At this age, you can't work in a company like other blacks do.'

'Yes,' Foti responded. 'That is why I tell them all the time that in politics, financial prognostic is essential. There is always an end ahead of every African politician. Either set by rival parties, or set by rival colleagues of the same party. But this is what my wife and children seem not to understand.'

* * * *

An injunction order had just suspended BAKWA. Four of its journalists and its manager were also summonsed. They were accused of defamation of the mayor's character and also of breaking press laws.

The Governor was after Tanga. The mayor was after him, and so too was the police.

However and whatever they were saying, Hansel described Tanga as, 'The man who refreshes people's minds on freedom, the man an *upside-down* society needs.'

Professor Hansel loved Tanga and would always tune to BAKWA FM, after listening to BBC or CNN news. Sometimes in addition, he would invite Tanga for closed door talks.

It was eminent that Tanga would be detained soon. The mayor was thinking to finish with him for once and forever and to leave no traces.

Ten

There was a business magnet called Felix Akonte. He had started business by retailing nails and door hinges. Upon the years, he had expanded his business to a company known as Société Bonpi. Bonpi had closed down once when Felix took off his hands the business due to high taxes. But when other small scale businessmen encouraged him to incorporate the business with others under the name of Bonpi, it became the largest in the country. Bonpi was a company dealing with the distribution of building materials and other related goods. It boomed more than ever before and employed thousands of people.

Akonte was a stepbrother to Hansel. He was almost absent in politics though was close to many staunch militants of the SDF. For that reason, he was suspected of pumping money into the party. He was the main shareholder of Bonpi.

Angwe Ndi was the managing director. Though not involved in politics like before, he sympathised with the SDF. For that lone reason, he was suspected of also giving financial assistance to the party.

* * * *

It was a bright though wet April day. The sun was setting. A heavy Jeep approached Chief Petro's residence.

Fon Petro was a huge man with excessive appetites for big posts. His authoritative, commanding appearance expressed such an attitude.

He had just retired from work and was lying on a sofa and in a deep snore. On a stool beside him was a bottle of Beck's beer. His wife was in the room and his children far behind the house.

Perhaps he was dreaming of his earthly comforts. The gateman entered and shook him awake. He stretched himself in annoyance. As if he had been dreaming comfortably, he asked in a crocket voice, 'What do you want?'

'The mayor and some others are here,' said the gateman. 'Should I let them in?'

'No. It must be a big issue. Let them into the visitors' sitting room. I will be right there.'

Not too long, a man laboured behind a big stomach from a passageway, then into the visitors' sitting room. He was breathing with difficulties and was so uneasy.

The four political figures sat.

'The Lord Mayor,' shouted Chief Petro as if he wasn't informed about the mayor's presence.

'The indomitable chief in person…' responded the mayor stretching his hand to greet.

'You're right.'

Petro rushed out and dashed back. Then a houseboy entered a few minutes later with a tray of wine glasses and champagne flutes.

'There is champagne, wine, beer, fruit juice and others. What can my boy offer you to…?'

In chorus and in happy but crocket voices, they gave different choices.

'I need some beer for today not spirit,' Foti said.

'Only Beck's beer is available. Do you like it?'

'That's even much better.'

They all began to sip from various glasses. There, was the mayor, the Southwest campaign manager, Muna Siri, the Delegate of Education for the Southwest region, Fomba and the Southwest general manager for electricity, Jean Pierre.

Jean Pierre was popularly known as JP. He had been in the region since a decade.

Foti dropped his glass on the table and leaned backwards with his index finger on his beard.

'Chief, what do you think of the sponsors of the opposition?' he asked.

'What do you mean?' asked Chief Petro.

'I mean there are lots of threats from the militants who keep squandering large sums.'

'You're right. We need much money to persuade the people. Otherwise, we risk losing the stand especially in this subdivision.'

There was silence for some seconds. The campaign manager, Muna breathed heavily and sipped from his glass as if he wanted to add something.

'Chief,' he said, 'there are many strategies apart from serious campaigns.'

'Yeah…'

'I mean deal away with Bonpi.'

'How does that work?'

'Let's pursue them with high taxes and sue them for nuisance. You know, the company has just been yanked from crisis. The least interruption would possibly lead to a decline and people like Akonte and Ndi will go bankrupt. If these financial devils fall, the party within this subdivision too will fall.'

'That's a point. But you need to know that Bonpi has got one of the most radical lawyers in town.'

'That's right,' said the Foti. 'Let's just try and if it goes bad, we can wash mouths with cash. Know that they are no exception to the world economic down turn. This is the time to stop them.'

The Chief wanted the party in power to consolidate its stand. That was all. However, the mayor had several ideas in mind. He hated Professor Hansel and his brother Akonte. Both brothers had appreciated the way Tanga used to ask questions, digging out the veracity of issues.

'Leave everything to me,' said the Chief. 'I know what to do. The company has to close down… You also know there are rumours that Akonte has now forty nine percent shares of FertCo, a fertiliser company.'

FertCo had expanded and could even supply to some West African countries.

Both Bonpi and FertCo were the two largest private companies that employed thousands of people. That number was expected to double in two years. These two companies were formed in Tiko and had spread over the years to some other parts of the country.

* * * *

Professor Hansel condemned both high taxes on companies and such arrangements with tax directors. Yet, the game was the game. People had become addicted to paying taxes behind doors.

In a write-up, a lecturer wrote, 'Do we fold our arms and watch Chinese and others deal freely on trade while our home companies face high taxes and are declining daily?' Further, he wrote, 'Let the government encourage both foreign investors and home companies, and let the government be aware that encouraging foreign investors should not mean robbing the people on our streets and to free foreign investors from taxes. What price are we paying?'

The mayor left with his friends. As he thought, success was coming. He was still suffering from the cold of his son's death. Many questions were coming more and more from the journalists. All those questions were exposing all secrets.

* * * *

Foti went back home accompanied by Muna Siri, the campaign manager. He had contacted Kingsley on phone before reaching home. It wasn't long. Kinsley entered.

'Time is the most decisive factor,' said Muna.

'As the mayor has said, let's keep Tanga out of this race for once and forever. This will help stop our secrets being leaked out through his interviews.'

'It's for Kingsley to organise his boys, or we'll regret and pay a heavy price,' the mayor said. 'Tanga is no political figure, but a tight dredge. He is a talkative through which people can know the plans... 2011 is not far. Soon, we will begin serious election campaigns. He needs to quit the scene.'

The commissioner looked at them with hands folded. His mouth thinned and his head swayed from left to right. He was like contemplating. The mayor didn't like that waste of time.

'I must make you know one thing,' said the mayor. 'If someone wants to kill you, declare him an enemy and kill him first. We risk our various posts if Tanga, the Professor and others live.'

When the Foti talked of Hansel, the commissioner was dreaded.

'No,' said the commissioner. Hansel is a great man. Both national and international eyes are on him. For now, let us forget of him. That case is peculiar and needs a high strategic way to handle. We need to concentrate on the talkative now.'

'There shall be cabinet shake-up after elections. No one can give clear political prognostics. So we only need to clear the way hoping for the best.'

Foti's eyes were red. He knew how unpredictable politics had been over the years. Just as one could be appointed at any time, he or she could be kicked out at any time. Some could be relegated or stripped of their jobs. Some could as well later be yanked to top posts. Politics had become so unforeseeable.

The day was fast aging out and the three men needed to conclude. The doorbell buzzed. Kennedy entered and greeted.

'Please give us some time,' said Foti. Kennedy fell out.

'We need money for this project,' Kingsley said.

'What are you saying?' asked Muna. 'No one goes politically shopping without money. You know it. The problem is not money. The only thing we should reflect is how to accomplish the mission. Just give us your estimate and then we will get into the campaign package and pinch something from it.'

Then, Kingsley said in a parched voice, 'We can give these boys ten million and the mission will register enormous success.'

'If that be the case, they should have a one week plan if not less to do so.'

Muna and Kingsley soon disappeared into the approaching darkness. Kennedy re-entered and met his father in deep thoughts. 'Is there something wrong?' he asked.

'As usual,' responded his father. 'The papers keep up with various reports. Some describe our militants as murderers. I would like to propose that you leave the country as fast as possible.'

Kennedy was silent with his bunch of keys jingling in his hand and his left elbow on his knee.

'Kennedy,' he said in a low voice, 'now is the most critical moment. You need to be agile. You need to be wise and vigilant. You need to walk carefully because these fools can efface your name from this life. Where is Williams?' The word *Williams* couldn't leave his mind as he shook his head and squeezed his eyes.

Foti's wife entered and stood for several seconds, unheeded. She was also still in the agony of the death of her son. 'What is the bad news?' she asked.

'Advise your son to leave this country immediately. The political atmosphere is lurked with evil. I can feel it.'

Kennedy was mute in a total mode of despair. What comforts a man, so rich like the mayor, if he suddenly lives without a family? His two daughters were absent. Williams was killed and Kennedy soon to leave for Europe. In the realm of politics, the environment was fierce and unpredictable.

Several minutes later, Kennedy yawned and looked at his father.

'What then? Is there any objection?' he asked his son emphatically.

'Well, not really, just that I will miss you all.'

'Better to be out of sight and to meet again than be in sight and later never to meet.'

His mother interrupted, 'Get what your father is saying. I know you will miss friends and business here but you can still be a big businessman there. The most essential thing in life is money which you do have even in excess.' She was just like her husband. To her, money was the answer to all things. After all, her husband had always succeeded in making money the answer.

Before the family left for bed, they were certain of a point. Kennedy would apply for a business visa. He would leave for Germany and would not come back so soon.

* * * *

At about 9 am the following morning, there was rowdiness at the Tiko central city.

'Burn him! Burn him!' shouted an angry crowd. Armed robbers had broken into one of the main distribution shops of Bonpi and left with a huge sum of money late in the night, the previous day. The police was informed. They chased and caught one of the bandits as he hit his car beyond repairs. The robber was locked up in the Tiko police cell. Many people in Tiko had often been victimised. News spread fast around that a robber was under police protection. The Tiko population stormed the police cell early that morning. Officers on duty couldn't stop them.

The angry crowd squeezed out the robber and carried him in the air, then slapped him on the highway. He was brutally stripped naked and his hands tied behind.

Blood oozed from his mouth and nose. Fast boys gathered car tyres and were eager to put him down to ashes by covering him with tyres and burning him. It was obvious that the immediate plan to burn him was going to be irreversible.

'Confess all your crimes and sins,' shouted a boy with excellent muscles.

'Yes, let him say all things he has been stealing and all the women he has raped,' supported the crowd in loud voices.

Just this time, a military truck approached from a far end. It was packed with soldiers on their way to the Bakassi peninsular, oil rich and disputed area.

The truck driver saw the crowd and slowed. One of the soldiers jumped down. 'What is the problem?' he asked.

Many were scared because the soldiers were more terrifying than the gendarmes and the police, often aggressive in all actions even when settling differences amongst themselves.

'It's a robber caught stealing from Bonpi,' said one of the onlookers.

The soldier took out his dagger and rushed to the robber. He frightfully cut off the robber's ear. The crowd applauded, though some people stamped hands on faces in fear. The soldier wiped his dagger on the robber and with the dexterity of an acrobatic monkey, jumped back onto the truck.

Other soldiers on the truck applauded. The truck recklessly kicked off.

The crowd continued shouting for him to confess. In tears, he named some of the big business places they ever broke into. He named a few people they shot dead and two women they once raped to dead.

A taxi driver arrived. He parked his car about two hundred metres away and approached the scene.

'Is this not Gabriel Tah!' shouted the driver.

'Do you know him?' asked one of the street boys holding fuel ready to pour it on the robber.

'He used to be a police constable at the capital city but was dismissed three years back for selling his service pistol.'

The boys were more annoyed and moved. About fifteen tyres surrounded and pegged him in the middle. Fuel was poured and another smart boy set it on fire. The whole city came out to witness Gabriel burnt to ashes.

Within a few minutes, only some dark substance was seen at the spot. Gabriel was no more. Gendarmes arrived at the scene followed by the Divisional Officer. The boys escaped. Some three hours later, the prisoners were brought to clean and bury the ashes of Gabriel.

The Lord Mayor condemned the act, saying that, 'All humans, no matter their crime, have the right to live.' He promised to arrest any further jungle justice executors. Whatever he was saying had no effect. The job was done and the boys were ready to do more.

Eleven

Months later, BAKWA TV was handling a business program. Tanga was at the front while others sat facing him. Among them were economic analysts, a professor in Economics and Management… There, was also Professor Hansel, Barrister Late, business consultants and some other important personalities. Most of them were neutral in politics. They sat discussing on the economic situation of Cameroon in particular and Africa as a whole.

'… This is disgrace,' said Professor Hansel. 'How do we fold our arms and watch these two mighty companies that employ over twenty thousand desperate Cameroonians close down?'

His eyes were red and full of suspect. Tanga looked at him with his right hand on his jaw.

'Alright,' he continued. 'Let me just read this article in the newspaper by a university student: *Men in political glad rags, because of political bias, and power mongering, have decided to close down companies, a means to derail plans of rival parties.* What do you have to say Professor?'

Hansel moved his head from one participant to the other. He sighed in annoyance and then said, 'Why are these heavy taxes and penalties pressed on these two companies only now that elections are coming up? What conclusions do we give when only these private companies are declining? Rather than the government encouraging by subsidising them, has decided to allow the taxation department force them to close down. Why should foreign business men feel free in this country at the expense of our young business strugglers?'

'Sorry, Sir. Let me not cut you short,' interrupted Tanga. 'What foreign business men do you mean?'

'Look around. You see Chinese with the biggest shops in this country. They enjoy free trade. If you look at their products in this country, you will agree with me that in the next one decade, we will have to employ bulldozers to clean our streets. Our country has been taken as a wastebasket where all cheap and poisonous products are dumped.'

Professor Hansel was cross. He was a man of the books. He was not too politics inclined but would always comment on any political wrongdoing from any of the parties. All he wanted was the respect for human rights and the practice of true democracy.

One of his idiosyncrasies was anger. The smallest thing could cause him to use his tongue anyhow and sometimes even wrongly. He could say any secret no matter what people would say whenever he was angered.

Tanga didn't want him to continue. 'And what advice do you want to give to the taxation department?'

'Well, I am not an economic expert like my learned colleague there,' he said raising his hand to Motala, a professor in Economics and Management. 'But let those who are in charge know that we are in a democratic world. Every individual has the right to belong to a party of his choice. If taxes are now used as a ploy to battle and to derail rival parties, this is not only a hideous and diabolic way to maintain one party in power, but it would be sheer dictatorship... Get it right that most government companies have been privatised and now, a few private companies are closing down. Just try to forecast the nearest future and you will find this country's economic and political future in clear jeopardy.'

Tanga flipped a few papers in his file and turned his head to Professor Motala.

'Now,' he continued, 'we take a one minute break and when we come back, we will be listening to Professor Motala.'

According to various private newspapers, there had been political fumbling and frustration in the whole country. Taxes climbed to about thirty percent. Other newspapers carried headlines such as: *Number of School Drop-outs has Increased. Fuel Prices Triple. Moss Plant Grows on Many Abandoned Cars.*

The one-minute music interlude was over and the TV screen changed to the learned group.

Tanga said, 'Welcome back. The topic of discussion is, *Taxes and the Sinking Economy*. Here with us is Motala Edward. He is Professor in Economics and Management and author of two books. Professor, once more you are welcomed.'

'Thanks,' responded Motala.

'Companies are closing down. Jobs are axed daily and taxes remain on a speedy increase. Also, foreign businessmen are custom duty freed. What is your opinion?'

'One of the ways to create jobs easily is to subsidise small firms and companies. This goes by way of reducing taxes or direct financial assistance. The government can't swallow the whole learned population into the public service. It is but obvious that when companies collapse, unemployment increases. That of Cameroon has reached its peak and nobody seems to do anything about it… Embracing foreign businessmen without taxing them is, maybe, to rescue our dropping economy.

First and foremost, on this issue, there is no way one can reconcile the act of allowing the Chinese and many others enjoy free trade but at the same time increasing taxes on domestic companies to above thirty percent. The issue of taxes on companies such as Bonpi, FertCo, and some others that has seriously threatened our economy is supposed to be a call for concern. The ruling party has to prove to the people that it has no hand in closing down these companies by resuscitating them. I am not out to back up rival parties in their allegations but at the same time, I haven't heard any government owned radio or TV station raising alarm for such a crisis.

Allegations or no allegations, acceptance of responsibility or not, let the government listen to the cry of its people. Cameroon is desperate. It is in a deep crisis. Let us join hands together and rescue the situation.

Secondly and most importantly, it isn't healthy for the government to give total freedom for the importation of all sorts of goods in the name of encouraging foreign businessmen. If we have to assess some of the goods that enter this country, we will regret. There is no refusal that some of the goods are of quality. Nevertheless, there is undisputable market poisoning. Goods banned all over Europe and America is what we accept in our country.

There are no prospects that this country shall have a single recycling company even in the next fifty years to come. What shall we do with the billions of heaps of metals and other trash dumped at roadsides? Our eco system is heavily threatened.

Tanga intervened, 'So what advice are you giving to our tax management and especially the government?'

'I am not here to give any advice because our tax officials have refused to countenance any proposal.'

'So, do we fold our arms?'

'We voice out our grievances to our lawmakers and to our ministers. They carry it in forms of bills to the parliament for debates. There are considerations, acceptance and finally passed as laws. So if we propose, no one cares to take it there, or when taken to parliament and is often voted out by the majority ruling party, how do you want us to fight? Or maybe go to the streets? No. We all know the consequences of upheavals. Demonstrators will be shot at, or at the end, this country will be like Sudan, Somalia, Liberia…'

'Professor, what do you have to say about Chinese even becoming hawkers on the streets pushing away our local youths, especially the Bamileke… The other day, the Bamileke women were on the streets calling on the Chinese to leave small size businesses for them.

'Leave or to reside here is not my business or any call for concern. We are not here to talk about racism faced by Africans in China or other parts of the western world as some of the demonstrators voiced the other day. We are talking about decisions taken by our top government and tax officials…'

'Your last words on free trade, Sir.'

'Let it be clear that none of the developed nations achieved its economic status through free trade policies. Also note that South Korea leaped from developing economy to a developed one through policies that ran counter to free market principles. Only the west gains from free trade at the expense of our local traders. So, let me end by repeating that what we want on the African continent is fair trade and not free trade which goes to increase the business bags of foreign traders. I would really want to reiterate that change in our loved and peaceful Cameroon will come from within and not from the west. More emphasis I would love to make at this point is that Cameroon like any other African country does not need any foreign donor. We only need foreign investment that hinges heavily on fair trade.'

'Thanks Professor,' said Tanga. 'It was nice having you all this week on the program. Don't miss next week's new edition. Don't forget that it will be special as we will have economic experts from Ghana…'

* * * *

The following day, the streets were busy. There were women with baskets of doughnuts, groundnuts, corn, and fruits. Some of them saying, 'Buy sweet corn,' or 'Buy one take two,' all these, to draw attention. There was high music emanating from small shops at roadsides, especially religious sounds from shops owned by the Nigerian hustlers.

The Chinese hustlers too were on the streets with their tricycles and the carriages with assorted chewable.

Almost none of them could speak English or French. They could be heard with words such as, 'fity,' meaning fifty francs, or 'cenkant,' meaning cinquante (fifty), in French. They never cared what names the local population gave them. They were courageous, as the authorities had given them the audacity to do business. They would condemn the goods of local women claiming that such goods were exposed and contaminated. They had a reason because theirs was well sealed. Because of that, they were making great progress.

* * * *

It was 6 pm that day. Tanga had stopped lodging at Che Hotel. He would only do so at Hotel Kom. Kom was the name of the owner of the hotel and he was the founder of BAKWA FM.

At 6.30 pm, two men in sober suits entered the hotel gate with briefcases. They walked straight to the reception where they met a lady.

'Good evening, Lady,' greeted one of them.

'Thanks, Sirs. Can I help you?'

'Yes, we are Lawyers from Yaoundé.'

'Yes. And you want to lodge with us, I suppose.'

'You're right, Madame.'

When the lady asked for their national identity cards, one of them said, 'Sorry, we don't have. But here are our cards.' They presented their professional cards to her.

'Same room?'

'Yes.'

The Lady took the register and said, 'Do you want a room up on a higher floor or down?'

'What is the difference?'

'Floor two is for VIPs like you,' she said with a smile.

'Second floor then. Thank you.'

She took them there.

On the table was a booklet with rules and regulations on how to get other services like food or call ladies.

Most people were controlled at the gate before entering into the hotel. However, men appearing to be diplomats like them were often allowed by the gate men. So when they arrived at the gate, the security boys said in chorus, 'Welcome, Sirs,' motioning their hands for them to go in. Surveillance cameras had nothing to do with weapons, but were just there to check the number of people going in and out. It was also to examine the suspects. Thus, the two men went in without any much control.

Two years back, a business magnet was alleged poisoned in the same hotel. However, lawyers set the defendants, including the hotel owner free from any responsibilities and succeeded in a civil party counter claim.

Tanga had been living on the second floor for a few days.

Security men would walk up and down the hotel to make sure all was in order. Four of them ascended and after a few minutes, they were heard hoofing down and then towards the gate. At this time, the two lawyers opened their door and walked to Tanga's hotel room and rang at the door. Tanga opened without any hesitation. 'Come in,' he said walking to the table with a newspaper in his hands. Before he could raise his head, a pistol was pointed on his forehead ready to be triggered. Tanga was relaxed. He took it to be a joke. He thought they were out to harass him for money.

'Don't move,' said one of them in a low deep voice. The other person added, 'Don't also talk.'

They closed the door. This time, he felt a different spirit.

'Please,' Tanga said in a slow hopeless voice, 'don't kill me.'

'Why?'

'Please, how much money do you want from me? I can give it all.'

'Shut your mouth. We don't need your fucking money. We have been paid to deal with you. We need your life. You are a heckler.'

'I am sorry, Sirs. Please, don't kill me.'

'Your last words… We have to kill you now.'

Tanga couldn't say another word as the man fired into his mouth. He only mumbled as he farted and messed in his trousers. His head was bleeding blood. Some blood made its way to the door, and then out into the corridor. The two men walked fast downstairs. When they approached the receptionist, they walked slowly. She looked at them and asked, 'Are you out for a walk?'

'Just to take some air around,' they responded.

Gently and audaciously, they walked out of the gate and none of the security officers questioned them as they disappeared into darkness.

About some twenty minutes later, the person next door to the deceased blew the alarm. He had heard the killers from his room though it wasn't all that clear. The security rushed up and opened the door. They met the deceased already stiff. The whole building was surrounded and investigations started.

Tanga was cold. He was never to be heard again. The veteran journalist, an eloquent reporter was no more.

The Hotel ambulance rushed the body to the hospital but unfortunately, the doctor confirmed he was dead.

The days became so cruel and fickle. Even though most sympathisers of the ruling party hated Tanga, there was a general cry the following morning for strict investigations. People were shocked. Early in the morning, all ears were tuned to the radio.

There was high tension. Both the gendarmes and police were on high alert. That same day, all security officers and the receptionist at the Kom hotel were arrested. There was great suspicion that two lawyers must have connived with any of these people to kill Tanga.

Heavy doubts came when the police found out that the names entered as Barrister Kinde and Dekin were never found on the Cameroon Bar list where names of all lawyers could be found. That was the beginning of the obscurity. The corpse remained at the hospital mortuary.

Guns had become a necessity. Men of the underworld were with guns, public security officers with guns, business tycoons with guns, everybody wanted to be with a gun. Why?

The youths were perishing. Icons, veterans and also mavericks too were perishing daily. Society was going empty. Society was in peril.

Feeble investigations into Tanga's death went on. All those arrested were released. There wasn't any backing that any of them was connected to the killing of Tanga.

Twelve

Weeks counted. It was a Monday morning and the airport was full with passengers. Kennedy is dressed this day in a dusty dark suit and ready to leave for Germany.

At the airport were people with trays of boiled eggs, groundnuts, cola nuts, jewellers, gamblers and many others, all of them struggling to survive. People were as busy as ants.

Kennedy was already inside the first checkroom for visa control. Those outside could watch them through a large glass window. His mother stood outside waving with a big smile. Kennedy stood behind a young man of about twenty-three years. The young man's passport was checked repeatedly.

'Young man,' asked a police officer, 'is this your passport?'

'Yes Sir.'

The passport was taken to two other police officers. They all shook their heads in disagreement. A call was made and suddenly, two other officers came in and said to the young man, 'You are under arrest.'

'Why, Sir?'

'You have tempered with the passport. It is not yours.' They handcuffed and took him away.

Ten minutes later, he appeared again from outside with a Lieutenant. Epaulets on the lieutenant's shoulders could explain how powerful he could be. He was huge and appeared to be of high security command.

On the right at the control room was a small corner demarcated with ceiling boards for dumping of cargo that wasn't allowed to be taken along.

The Lieutenant didn't respect the queue. He walked straight to the police officers. They gave him a military salute.

'Excuse me,' he said to them and one of them followed him to the tiny corner. The boy stood waiting with a hateful face. Two minutes passed. The lieutenant was about to leave. The boy and the police officers thanked him joyously. From their faces, there had been an immense compensation. No one knew what discussion took place at the corner but for sure, something had happened.

The police looked at the passport again. 'What happened to your own passport?'

'I have never had one. I just bought it.'

'Well, watch out at the airport in France. Otherwise, the police will seize this pass and repatriate you.'

He took back the passport and thanked them so immensely. He was directed to the small path leading to the plane.

Kennedy and the new friend were directed in. They walked so relaxed and confident. They were not the type with doubted passports. The plane was humming and passengers were listening to safety instructions.

When the plane took off, Kennedy was dizzy. He soon closed his eyes. Some ugly unshaped thoughts came to his mind.

'Wow,' he thought. 'This is just like a journey from one planet to the other. Why all these? This is really a cock and a bull story. Is it just because my parents are daredevils?'

He woke from his sleep and wiped his face with a disposable handkerchief. Okafor was just next to him. He watched him. 'I am feeling dizzy,' he said to him.

'Yes it's like that sometimes.'

For some length of time, Kennedy spoke no word. Okafor noticed that Kennedy was worried.

'Is Germany a nice place to live?' asked Kennedy.

'Well,' he responded, 'it is good but sometimes could be so stressful and frustrating.'

'How?'

'Emmm…' doubted Okafor not knowing what to say.

'You mean hard life? I hear it has a strong economy.'

'You're right. But men like you and I won't be fortunate.'

'How?'

'Their money circulates within the economy and laymen like us have limits to have it, or to have good jobs like them. The whole thing turns to be modern slavery. Are you going for some business stuff?'

'Yes… I want to study the environment and to carry out some investments there. Home is becoming cruel.'

'I know. But running from home problems to the western world is to have a life between the devil and the deep see.'

'Really? What do we do then? At least it should be better over there.'

'Kennedy, believe me. The western world is facing serious crisis in addition to the fact that a black man needs to get back to build his home. Running to the west now is like a drowning hunter holding a sinking ship.'

Kennedy looked at Okafor with some hatred. But the seriousness on his face seemed to have expressed some veracity.

Though Kennedy had often read some of the western papers on foreign maltreatment, he used to interpret them to be political. Some other times he thought those suffering in the western world were poor refugees with no capital to carry on some investments. He thought for some time and asked, 'Are there no great Africans there, even one? So do you mean to say people don't make it at all?'

'It is total rubbish.'

'And what job do you do there?'

'I wash plates in a restaurant, if that is what you want to hear. Unfortunately, most businesses are facing a collapse. We Africans are failing in building our continent and the consequences is that we will continue to be slaves to the Whites. If we don't do something, we will wash their toilets for the rest of our lives.'

Kennedy hated him for that. He interpreted it to be an aspect of hopelessness. He winked in thoughts. Such words from Okafor were the kind of common sense he never thought of.

'Why not stay back home too? You can also build the community.'

'That's true,' replied Okafor. 'I have a child there and I've equally worked for some years. It is hard to take a spontaneous decision going back home, though I still have to endeavour. Let me tell you that my own case isn't the worst. Do you know how many billions of money our people are siphoning to western banks? Why not steal and invest in your own country? Our politicians are lunatics.'

Kennedy didn't want to listen to the shit anymore. He took a newspaper from Okafor and they diverted their minds to it. It was a safe journey to France and then to Germany.

Thirteen

Kennedy passed the night at a Düsseldorf train station with the police. He handed them his particulars and they took his fingerprints as he declared himself a refugee. Early the following morning, a police car drove him to the German Federal office in Düsseldorf, North West of Germany to start an asylum process.

A different life began. That day, there were about a hundred new asylum seekers. They all stood outside the building queuing for asylum declaration forms to fill. When given forms, they were asked to get into the hall and were ushered to various seats waiting for more questions. There was more questioning, fingerprint confirmation, explanations on how the asylum interview would proceed.

To Kennedy, it was a lacklustre stuff. On the very first day, they were given one Euro each for telephone calls, which Kennedy didn't really need. They were also given small plastic bags with some little sandwiches.

After midday, a lady came to them and said, 'It is over for today. You have to descend and get into the buses out there. We will take you to where you will pass the night. There, you will have further explanations on how your asylum process will run.'

Some would be interviewed the following day, while others would have to wait a week or two, like Kennedy.

From the German Federal office *Bundesamt*, they were taken to a ship anchored near the River Rhein. The ship seemed to have been there for some two decades. This could be testified from the moss plant around it.

The ship was called an asylum hotel. It contained about four hundred tiny rooms. There was a larger room meant for eating and watching television. Those who had no appointment could sit the whole day watching news and music.

At the entrance of the hotel was a receptionist. He was to receive and study papers of new persons. He saw Kennedy well dressed and it gave him some special attention. 'Welcome, Sir,' he said to Kennedy. 'You are new. Am I right?'

'Yes, Sir.'

He looked at the papers for some time and said, 'You will have your interview on Thursday.'

'Yes, Sir.'

'Alright, I will give you some bedding now and show you where to pass the night until your interview and subsequent transfer to a transit camp.'

It was 8.30 am on Thursday. Kennedy sat in a waiting room expecting an interview. Most of the asylum seekers were from the West African coast. There were also some white Arabs, but they were not as desperate as those from west and east Africa. Asylum seekers were called to various rooms. Most often, the interviewer was one versed with the political situation of the seeker's country of origin.

A lady walked and stood at the door. She opened and read from a file, 'Kennedy Foti.' Kennedy indicated with his hand while rising from his seat.

'Please come with me. You have your interview today. Are you ready for it now?'

'Yes, Madame.'

Within a minute or two, he was ushered to sit in front of a frightful man. The huge figure mumbled a few words and then read from a file. The lady translated to him, 'I am the interviewer. The lady sitting here will translate to you in English. You will be asked questions on why you decided to leave your country, and you are going to answer them.'

The interviewer was as big as an elephant. He was breathing forcefully as if too much fat was blocking his nose. He yawned and stretched himself, seeming exhausted. Just on his right, pasted on the wall was the map of Cameroon. There were also other documents for reference.

For over an hour, the interview continued. He would ask questions and later come back to them.

'You said the opposition party killed your brother and now they also want to kill you.'

'Yes, Sir.'

'Talk maturely. The opposition party is not a single person. Am I right?'

'Right, Sir.'

'Can you name those who wanted to kill you and any of the occasions?'

'I escaped an assassination attempt one Saturday on my way back home. I couldn't identify them.'

'That means you don't know who wanted to deal with you that Saturday since you could not identify any body. Is that right?'

Kennedy was mute and seemed lost. His head fell though his eyes still focused on the huge figure just in front of him. He was seeing and hearing the opposite of his imaginations. It was hard for someone like Kennedy that had often been a figure of serious command back home to be commanded and pressurised. The interviewer heaved backwards. He wasn't convinced.

'You know what,' he said, 'you have to say the truth with detailed convincing facts. Otherwise, you have to leave this country with immediate effect.' Kennedy felt intimidated. Still, he said nothing. The interviewer took a stick of cigarette and said, 'You can relax for some five minutes.'

The interpreter took him out to the waiting room. The meaty interviewer opened the window. As he sucked from his cigarette and sent out the smoke in bubbles, the lady hoofed back at a brisk pace.

'Smoking?' she asked.

'Yeah,' he responded.

She took two cubes of chocolate from a plastic plate on the table and began to suck too.

'Do you think he is faithful in his narrations?' asked the interviewer.

'Yes. I think so.'

'Why?'

'There is some aspect of truth in it. He has handed over his passport, birth certificate, and savings book. Though he's childish in his arguments, but I think…'

'Why do you think he has such a big amount in the bank?'

'If really his father is a mayor, then it is possible. I know the culture of most African administrators.'

'It is really a big sum. If converted, it is something above nine hundred thousand Euros.'

The interviewer repeated the amount several times. He drank from his glass, sucked again from his cigarette and dropped the remains in an ashtray on the table.

'Ask him to transfer the money now to Germany.' That idea went straight into his head. 'If the son is so rich, then the father can be a multibillionaire, and we need this money,' he thought.

The interviewer appeared greedy as a wily old fox. He was a hog in character and in size too. Thirty minutes had passed. He looked at the documents on his table, and starred again at the photocopy of the passport.

'Call him in,' he said to the lady. She dashed out, and in a minute, Kennedy was in.

'… What if we decide to deport you?'

'Well, I can't tell. But I think that my life will be in danger.'

'What if we decide to grant you a stay?' When asked this question, he was silent for several minutes. He mumbled and almost smiled but said nothing in response. He felt a sense of freedom and relaxed a little.

'What of your money back home? How protected is it?'

'For now, I know it is in a protected place.'

'If the German government doesn't take care of you, how do you manage yourself?'

'I can receive money from home or transfer my account over here if that could be accepted.'

The frizzy face of the man smoothened. He was not as bitter as before.

Kennedy could realise it but couldn't give it any interpretation. He too became courageous, determined and hopeful in his arguments.

The interviewer was going over the jottings he had been making.

Kennedy stayed in same place thinking to himself.

Back home, Kennedy used to be as rich as his father and late brother. It was not out of meritocracy, but out of his father's status as the mayor of Tiko.

The interviewer prepared the recorded interview and played it for Kennedy to listen. 'We have to play this to you now. You'll listen to what you have told us. If there are any changes, you have the right to adjust them.'

It played and he listened to it all and then signed as a confirmation. The interviewer added, 'Please, do not hesitate to contact the banks if you feel like transferring your money to this country. It is your right to do so.'

The lady led him back to the waiting room. At the passageway, she halted and said, 'You don't have to worry. Your application for asylum will be granted.'

'Do you think so, Madame?'

'I am sure.'

'Well, if you say so.'

All his documents, including bank booklet were handed back to him.

* * * *

Later that day in the hotel, most asylum seekers sat watching television. Some were narrating their stories to others. According to the stories, some came by plane. Others said they made their way through Morocco and then struggled to Spain and finally entered Germany.

The debut of the twenty first century was that of foolhardy adventures. Both the poor and the rich were escaping from Africa into Europe. Administrators were making Europe their banks.

The desperate asylum seekers discussed topics such as Neo Nazism and foreigners, discrimination, racism, Obama to change the world, and many others. When Obama became president, it gave everyone the courage and the mind that all things are possible. *Yes We Can* became a slogan for every struggling man.

Days were counting. Asylum seekers were transferred every day to transit camps. They would wait for another period of three months for the treatment of their applications.

Kennedy had no transfer yet. He waited for weeks and became tired. However, he kept on. For this while, he was dreaming every night. He had dreams that his mother was no more. Though he called home several times, he was sure that something was at a countdown. Kennedy started going out for a walk with others, though not often. He could do so once in two days.

Fourteen

Kennedy and two others were taking a walk. They wondered if the crowd they saw approaching was on demonstration. They also doubted if they were simply people in celebration.

'What could be such an anniversary? Are they Germans?' Then a friend responded, 'For sure, they are Germans.'

There were over three thousand Germans in black dresses. Most of them had piercings all over their bodies, some having more than three earrings on one and the same ear. They equally had frightful tattoos. Over a hundred police officers stood watching them in their demonstration. Their songs were in German. 'Ausländer raus… Müssen raus.' They meant that all foreigners must leave. Any time such demonstrations were up, all foreigners would try to avoid passing near them. If they must do so, the paramilitary police often guarded them. The demonstrators were ready to fight and die, even though some of them had no reason why they wanted foreigners to leave. All they knew was that their brothers were on the streets and they needed to support them.

This twentieth century practice was transcending into the twenty first century and even more.

Some countries like Great Britain, France, and the USA passed harsh laws to buttress the fight against racism. Germany wasn't showing any serious concern. Rather, over the years, there had been a serious deportation of foreigners to their various countries of origin.

Kennedy didn't take the slogans of the demonstrators seriously. Not because he didn't want to, but because something else occupied his mind. He could only think of his asylum case and his colossal sum of money back home. They walked passed the crowd. The stubborn boys continued with their hullabaloo words. The boys looked at them with lots of threats. As they were some few meters away, they saw a young African on the ground. About ten boys on him, he was beaten seriously. The police intervened. This rather annoyed the demonstrators. They wailed in their songs: *Ausländer raus, nigger raus, alle raus, Müssen raus…* The uproar was high this time.

As the day was aging out, Kennedy found that the German society could be threatening. From this moment, a different image about the society he found himself began to germinate in his mind.

They were thirsty. 'We can drink something here,' said Kennedy pointing to a kiosk.

'We need to be careful,' responded a friend. 'Those boys can attack us here.'

The kiosk owner raised his head to them, 'Darf ich helfen?' he asked.

'Please, we don't understand German,' said Kennedy. 'Do you speak English?'

'A little bit.'

'We need some beer.'

They drank a bottle each. Kennedy paid and they continued along the beautiful streets of Düsseldorf. People were busy. As they walked, many people could understand they were new from their walking attitudes. Three men stopped them. Embarrassment! They were in faded jeans and appeared to be low class men. No one could predict that any of them could be a police officer. One of them whipped a card from his chest pocket and said pointing it to them, 'Criminal Police.'

'Are we criminals?' one asked.

'Not that. Can we see your passports?' They panicked somehow. It was embarrassing and intimidating. Kennedy was so uneasy. They had no option but to present the documents they had.

'You are asylum seekers.'

'Yes, we are.'

The environment and the people all seemed weird. To him, this was a serious negative impression. He was a calm man, though it was due to naivety. The police officers were off. He began to think heavily as they walked. He thought of how the Ibo boys from neighbouring Nigeria were often brutalised by the Cameroon police officers. It was at this time that he could imagine what a foreigner could face in a strange land. He thought of the time when his father took control of the Tiko council, and drove away some of the business Ibo boys who couldn't pay their dues to the council. Some others had their huts dismantled by council orders.

* * * *

They soon reached the hotel. From outside, he saw the receptionist holding a piece of paper. He had just received a fax. As they passed in, he asked, 'Hello, who is Foti Kennedy?'

'I am Foti, Sir.' He answered expecting to hear more.

'I have just received a fax. It is for you. You have to report to the Federal Office early tomorrow morning.'

'Any problem, Sir?'

'I don't think so. I think it concerns your application for asylum.'

He heaved a sigh and looked at his friends. He thought his case was going badly. Many had had their transfers but he still lingered there. It was easier for them to deport him because he handed them his passport. However, he remained silent and was ready to face it.

That evening, after dinner, they sat watching television before bed. They watched the Spanish police interrogating illegal immigrants caught crossing from Morocco into Spain. Such images were so disgusting. African immigrants knew the stories of ending their lives in western restaurants and toilets but they made up their minds. They needed it so madly. They had no choice. To Kennedy, the story was quiet different. He was still thinking big. He had the capital to start big business. Until this moment, he was still a big guy. Money speaks, he used to think.

* * * *

Early in the morning, they took breakfast and took off for the Federal office.

While at the sitting room, a lady hoofed from a passageway and called Kennedy. As they walked, she turned and shook hands with him.

'How did you sleep, Mr.Foti?'

'Fine.'

'We have been handling your application for asylum, so you will get the result today.'

He was quiet. They walked on slowly as the lady watched him. There was no happiness. She could find for herself that Kennedy was in doubts and despair.

'You need not fear. Just be hopeful.'

She took him to the same room where he had had his interview. The person on duty wasn't the one that interviewed him.

'Have a seat please,' said the man.

'Thanks.'

The lady that came with Kennedy was an interpreter. She introduced the man and then explained why they called him in.

It was rare that decisions for applications for asylum could come within a few days. Kennedy's case was unique. Most cases could take years and at the end, decisions were often negative. Once negative, the applicants were to leave the country within a few days or months. Others who hesitated were taken to deportation camps and sent back home.

They read to him all the information about what he had given to them: date of birth, his names, parents' names and address, account information and the approximate amount in it. After that, he signed as a confirmation.

'We are satisfied with your application,' said the man. 'After all necessary investigations, we found it convincing to grant your application for asylum. You have the right to stay in Germany. Also, you have the right to transfer your money to any of our banks.'

Thereafter, there were further explanations on how they would assign him to a residence. After that, he would make a choice of where to stay in Germany.

Kennedy was soft spoken. He hardly showed emotions. He didn't even thank them or show any sign of peculiar sudden change of behaviour.

'Do you have any question?'

'Not really. But I just want to ask if there is a limit.'

'What limit do you mean?'

'I mean a limit to the amount of money I can transfer.'

'Not at all. Transfer any amount you wish. Rest assured that your money would be in the best hands. There is also the right to withdraw your money at any time you want.'

A week later, Kennedy was in his new apartment. At least, Europe was smiling on him. To him success was clear and the first thing that came to his mind was for his father to pay him a visit. At this moment, his father's political stance was at a peril.

Upon the years, his father's political education made him know that a public figure was not for maintenance of dignity. A politician wasn't out to maintain long term values or to have continuous admiration. Foti made his children know that political success was financial success. This caused him to have many foes in life. These days, Kennedy was thinking out his brain more than ever. Whenever a man grows big, his problems too do grow. When money comes, it does so with many troubles.

However, Kennedy mumbled alone in a cracked voice, 'Better comes money with its accompanying problems than to die as a church rat and a no problem man.'

Although Kennedy never killed to have money, he knew his father's hands were stained.

Fifteen

He wasn't long without a girlfriend. His personality, social comportment and his financial ability made him a figure of attention. That is the reason he had a beautiful lady in the area he resided. Katrine Dasi had just broken out from a relationship. When it happened, she met with Kennedy in a shop and they exchanged telephone numbers. That was the beginning of their relationship.

Katrine was a Cameroonian too. She had been living in Germany for three years. She was beautiful and was also a tall figure of attraction. She wasn't the type of girl for men to stop easily. She thought age was working on her and was hoping to get married soon. On his part, Kennedy was not the rushing type on that and thought that it was too early to do so. That alone was giving them bitter faces.

* * * *

Some three weeks later, Kennedy was expecting his father. They were not on good terms that early morning as they sat for tea because they had some hard words in the night.

Back home, he would throw away any girl who gave him the least headache. He made it clear to her. That was the reason she would shout but later calm down.

They picked his father from Düsseldorf International Airport later that day. He was exhausted. From the airport to his apartment, father and son discussed nothing about money except the little discussion about the family. They spent the day together with Katy, but she didn't spend the night there with them. She went to her place and would be back early the next day.

Mayor Foti didn't find the western world too strange. He had visited many countries in Europe during his days as head coach of a first division football club. During this time, he resigned because a huge sum of money disappeared from the coffers, and he was heavily accused.

Katy came early in the morning and was in the kitchen making tea and some eggs for breakfast while Kennedy and his father waited while discussing.

'I hope she is a good housewife,' asked Foti in a mumble voice.

'It's not long since I knew her.'

'You can tell just for this short while. Don't trade with those that betray. Have you told her why I am here?'

'No, I haven't said anything to her. Why should I?'

'Women are beautiful but dangerous things. They can make the lowest things to rise and at the same time the highest things to fall. You have to trade with a woman only with your face but not with your heart.'

'I know, Dad.'

'Good then.'

Katy heard but didn't understand all they were discussing. She entered from the kitchen with a tray of tea cups, spoons, and napkins.

'Oh, my beautiful daughter,' said Foti. 'Is this how you've been comforting my son?' When he said so, he laughed and soothed Katy's hair as she was placing the saucers on the table.

She looked at Ken and thrust her tongue as if she doubted her way of setting the table. She smiled and dashed back to the kitchen with gay steps.

Foti was sandwiching his bread. He wanted to finish and knuckle immediately on business. He was becoming impatient. The more, he left the council for his deputy to control and was supposed to go back home so fast.

Breakfast was over. Katy was away for some minutes. Foti's hand suddenly supported his head. He looked into his son's eyes. 'Now tell me,' he said. 'What are the developments?'

'They granted my application for asylum as I told you on the phone, and I have just established a bank account.'

'Which banking institution is it?'

'It is Multiple Interest Bank which is MIB.'

'Is it ready now for money to enter from home?'

'Yes.'

Foti looked down on the floor without any precision. His eyes and mouth fumbled in an unsynchronised manner.

'Yeah,' he motioned his head. 'We have to direct Kingsley now to push some money into it without any delay. The rest will come gradually... or what do you think?'

'That is the point.'

'Is there any restriction on withdrawal?'

'As I know, all banks allow for withdrawals.'

'Kennedy, you are not a child. You should have made good findings. You have to be inquisitive.'

Kennedy was quite blunt as concerned the banking system of the country. He had a brief and nebulous counselling from the MIB bank advisers.

'Well,' Foti concluded in benefit of doubts, 'no one can really tell which financial institution is most secured when it comes to money.'

They were happy that something started. Foti had always told his son back home about saving money in Switzerland. 'I have to meet Batholo Nyah,' Foti said.

'Where does he live?'

'He lives in Switzerland.'

'Really?'

'Yes. He has been living there for many years now.'

'I don't really know much about Switzerland,' Kennedy said. 'All I know is that it is a neighbouring country to Germany and is a small country.'

'You are right. It is a west European country with a population of about seven million. You can look at the map. I think it should be to the south of Germany.'

Some African politicians had their money hidden in their banks. It was a pride for most politicians to have billions in such banks. Best Interest Bank (BIB) was the highest financial institution in Switzerland. It was best even around the whole of Europe. BIB was Foti's dream bank. Upon the years, the bank had been keeping top financial secrets.

Batholo was a friend to the mayor, and had fled home about five years back after a sex scandal with a five-year-old girl. The party in power equally accused him for being a political loud mouth. Since he left the country, their relationship was frail but now, they were reuniting. Batholo was helping him get answers to his financial consolidation in Switzerland.

Father and son were still at the table. 'So you know nothing about BIB?' his father asked.

'The only thing I know is that there is a big bank in Switzerland that takes all amounts and also keeps top financial secrets.'

'That is it, and it is the most important thing. Even if they don't give any interest, I don't care… So everything in Germany will continue to be in your name and that in Switzerland will be in my account.'

Back home, Foti fought several wars with the media, receiving support from his party big brothers. He was winning the war against journalists. Thus, his impromptu visit wasn't followed by any local radio station.

At this time, BAKWA FM was under an injunction order. Tanga was dead and the rigors of obscured and fatal scenes were now keeping young journalists and writers under control.

As Kennedy and his father discussed, his telephone beeped.

'Who is the person ringing?' Kennedy asked picking it up. 'Hello.'

'Hi, Ken. It's Desy.'

'How are you, Desy?'

'Fine, I was told that your father is around.' Foti didn't want people to notice he was there, and his son was quite aware. For that reason, he told Desy, 'I am on line. Please, can I call you in a few minutes?'

'Who was that?' his father asked.

'It's a friend.'

'A Cameroonian?'

'Yes.'

'You should and must be very cautious. Let no one estimate your financial strength. I say never.'

He pulled his chair closer. 'Young man,' he said, 'I want to advise you. Esprit de corps should be on your lips but let individualism of a peculiar flair define your daily activities especially when it comes to money.'

He paused and looked at Kennedy in his eyes. Don't sell your secrets by telling anyone that you have such a huge account. No matter how much you love this girl, don't let her know your situation.'

'Why should I? Am I a child?' Kennedy asked frankly.

'Good,' Foti continued. 'This is the plan. Kingsley will transfer all money from your account at home to this one. We have to give him a call today or early tomorrow because that same tomorrow I will be off for Switzerland.'

'When are you coming back, Dad?'

'I will be back in about three days. The council needs me.' At this time, Kennedy received a call from the US. Her sisters wanted to know how their father arrived.

Foti was ready to talk with his children. They were in the States already making life. Jacky was elderly to Quinter. Quinter had always been so bitter with his father for being heavily involved in politics. For Jacky, she didn't support her father being a politician nor hated him for being one. She was neutral, never taking side.

'Hi Dad,' said Jacky on phone. 'How was your journey?'

'I give praises to God! I arrived yesterday,' Foti said.
'I have just called Mum.'

'Yes, I know she is doing great.'

'But she must be lonely, Dad. You left her alone.'

'Say something important girl. Is she a child?'

'Some political talks, is that what you mean?'

'You are just being childish.'

He heard her suffocating in tears. 'Oh children,' he said perfunctorily and dropped the phone on the table as if it was a disturbing toy.

* * * *

It was only early the following day that the mayor discussed with Kingsley back home. A sum was to enter Kennedy's account as fast as possible. That same hour, he arranged with Batholo who would receive him. Things were moving smoothly.

Early the next day, the Lord Mayor was on board the ICE (Inter-city Express), a fast train. He hoped to talk with the BIB bankers that same day.

The Basel main train station where he was to drop wasn't far away from the BIB building.

Pushing money into the BIB was simple. Anyone around the world could do it, but the main problem was withdrawal, especially for African clients with unclear sources of income. Despite this problem, the influx of new customers from Africa was alarming.

* * * *

A 2006 story by a private newspaper narrated that the president of a French speaking West African country secretly deposited a few billions in BIB. One year later, the president was defeated in a presidential race. This time as a normal citizen, he dashed to BIB to withdraw the stolen money. The manager of BIB turned down the quest for withdrawal saying to former president Kokore Pierre, 'This account belongs to His Excellency, President Kokore Pierre of Lome and not to Mr. Kokore Pierre.'

The matter reached an impasse and Mr. Kokore involved international lawyers. His lawyers were ready to exercise their legal abilities. However, on the other part, BIB lawyers were more adamant. Kokore wasn't able to prove that the huge sum was savings from his monthly income.

The tiny republic of Lome was experiencing serious economic crisis. The Kokore case became too tough with no solutions to it.

Legal experts advised the people of Lome to organise fresh elections and to allow Kokore to win and come back to power.

The country organised elections in April 2007 and Kokore came out victorious. Second time president, Kokore, his prime minister, lawyers and some international organisations mounted pressure on BIB, and the huge amount returned to the Lome national treasury.

Both the national and international community heavily castigated the president. He made a public speech with explanation as to why he deposited such a vast sum in a western bank. When the president recovered the money, lawmakers passed and voted bills that the sum was for building more primary schools. President Kokore apologised to the public and swore that he would never do such a blind deal in his life.

* * * *

Basel train station was busy as usual. It was one of the biggest train stations in Europe with maximum security.

The mayor arrived. When he dropped from the train, he remained fumbling at the platform of rail 10A as all the tracks were numbered. He was descending and ascending the stairway. Batholo mistakenly heard of track 10E instead of 10A.

After about fifteen minutes of waiting, Batholo was sure he wasn't at the right place. He descended to the information office to ask for the time an ICE from Germany would arrive.

Down at the station, was a passageway just like a dredge under a bridge. There, were offices, small shops, police secret rooms, surveillance cameras, and private security offices that one could not easily identify.

Just near the information room, the mayor and Batholo saw each other. They embraced themselves and were about to move. The police had been monitoring Foti for all this while. Two police officers suddenly stopped them. Two others were approaching from a far end. They began to question them.

'Can I know you, Sirs, if you don't mind?'

'I am Foti Posh,' responded the mayor.

'Yes. Can I see your passports?'

They all handed their identification papers to the police officers. Foti's passport was an old one. It was a passport he used since the days when he was the coach of a football team. At this time, his picture was somehow different.

His look was a little bit fumbling. It wasn't for any fears of the police control but because he had something in his briefcase. There were doubts but the police were not in a haste to rush him up with many questions. They were relaxed.

'Good passport,' said one of the police officers holding it tightly. He looked at the mayor's briefcase. Batholo's identification card wasn't of any big concern. They concentrated more on the mayor.

'Hello Sir, we'll like to see your briefcase.'

'Am I a suspect?' he asked.

'No, it is for the safety of the people including you. You have arrived here safely because of our efforts to protect peoples' lives.'

He surrendered his briefcase. They opened it but closed it again briskly. Then in a low voice and closer to his ears, he said 'Sir, come with us to the office.'

When the police officer gripped the briefcase tightly, they didn't care much about the mayor escaping. They took some steps forward and the officer turned to him and fidgeted, 'Don't be scared. We need to protect you and what you are carrying.'

Batholo could understand what was going on because he already knew the reason of Foti's coming. The only thing is that he didn't know how huge the amount could be. However, to Batholo, it was an embarrassment. He didn't go with them. He stood there waiting for his friend.

In their office, they ushered him to a seat. Another officer stood at the door. In his briefcase were millions of banknotes, a traveller's cheque, and also some pieces of paper that he would collect money from the western union.

He watched at them as they searched his briefcase. His index finger moved up and down his jaws and his left hand supported his waist. He was like a captured criminal.

'Is this your money?'

'Yes, Sir.'

'Why did you decide to travel with such a big amount? And how did you pass all the check points without being discovered?' He was quiet for some seconds before clearing his throat to talk. 'It is my money. I just withdrew it from the bank before coming to Germany.'

'How and why was it not detected at all control points.'

'The inner bag protects it from being viewed by the cameras.'

'Why did you decide to carry the money with you?'

'Because it is not really in a safe place there and a friend advised me to establish an account with BIB.'

'Good, what do you do for a living?' One of them asked.

'I am the mayor of Tiko Subdivision of the Southwest region in Cameroon.'

'Do you want to go straight to BIB?'

'Yes, Sir.'

'Can we give you a lift?'

'What do you mean?'

'I mean we drive you to BIB.'

'Yes, Sir.'

Batholo saw them when they came out from the police office, slid into the police bus and took off towards BIB. They didn't give him the briefcase to hold. When they arrived at the bank, they handed the big sum to the bankers to count and establish an account for Foti. The police detached the inner black bag from his briefcase and told him they have the right to do so. When the bankers took hold of the briefcase, the police left.

The bankers explained to him the advantages of having a BIB account. They advised him not to carry physical cash with him but to establish an account in his country and do transfers to any BIB branch around the world.

He spent the night with Batholo and returned to Germany the following day. He was ready to fly back home.

Sixteen

Money was transferred into Kennedy's account from home. About a week after he had the money sent to his account, he went out with his girlfriend for a walk.

When he returned, something seemed to be going wrong in his apartment.

There was a flowerpot up near his window, hung to a nail. He realised that someone tempered with it in his absence. The main stem of the flower was broken. It wasn't the way he left it.

'Was someone here?' he doubted. Kennedy studied his things keenly. Up in his wardrobe, some documents were not the way he left them. 'I keyed my door. Who must have come here?'

Katy stayed behind for some little shopping. They had been all the time together. She soon entered.

'Why are you moving things up and down, Darling?' she asked. He explained to her and they all wondered.

The caretaker used to come for refurbishments in the absence of tenants but his apartment didn't need such repairs. Even if it was to be the case, they ought to have talked it out. He ascended to the caretaker's temporal door at an upper floor but there was no one there.

When Kennedy re-entered his room, he thought of the police because they were the only officers with the right to do so. Katrine entered the kitchen to make food. 'Please,' said Kennedy, 'make sure you wash every utensil you want to use there.'

'Yes, my Baby?'

'No one knows. We don't know who entered here and why.'

However, he soon dropped the idea and switched on his television. He watched music for about ten minutes, but those thoughts pursued him madly. He rose and walked to the wardrobe to check his MIB account card in his suit. He found it but was still so sceptical.

Katy knew Kennedy's financial situation was good even though she didn't know how too heavy it was.

He stoically abandoned himself on the sofa and continued to watch music absent minded.

'Darling,' she said sitting on his legs, 'are you so worried about what has happened?' Then she soothed his hair also watching music while her pot was on the cooker.

In the evening, Kennedy was sleeping heavily from the thoughts of the day. His telephone rang. He turned to a side cupboard and picked it. The identity of the caller didn't show. He dropped the phone without answering.

'Why don't you want to pick the call?' asked katy stretching herself. Kennedy was quiet. 'Who is calling you, Baby?' she insisted shaking him.

'Hey, don't bore me. I don't border about unknown callers.'

The phone started ringing again. Katy didn't hesitate to pick it up. It was Kennedy's father. He was home. She greeted him and handed over the telephone.

'Kennedy,' he said venomously, 'how dare you allow your telephone to be answered by a girlfriend?'

'I was sleeping, Dad.'

'Yes, but she was able to get up, a woman!'

After seconds of silence caught in guilt, Kennedy asked, 'How was your journey back?'

Foti didn't respond. He expected him to talk about something else. Rather, he asked, 'Is it in?' meaning the money that was transferred.

'What do you mean, Dad?'

'You see? Wake up from slumber. I mean the money.'

'Yes, everything is in order.'

'Alright, I am tired and need some rest.'

They ended the call. Kennedy and Katy huddled up and continued to sleep.

* * * *

The following morning, Katy got up earlier and prepared breakfast. She prepared the table and left. Kennedy was alone at breakfast when someone rang at the door. He waited for seconds but heard no voice. He damned it and continued with tea. The bell rang again followed by an aggressive knock.

He muted the television and listened. The bell rang again, four successive times.

He walked to the door with his cup of tea and watched through the peephole. Three men were standing at the door. He hesitated to open. They were convinced that someone was in. Possibly, they heard voices emanating from the television. When they attempted ringing again, he opened.

'Can I help you?'

'Good morning,' greeted one of them in an authoritative voice.

'Good morning,' responded Kennedy.

'Can we get in?'

'Why and who are you?' he asked with an aggressive face. One of them immediately showed him a small card. 'We are criminal police officers. You have a series of questions to answer from us. Is that alright?'

Kennedy didn't reply. He swayed his head from one face to the other. 'Am I a criminal?' he asked.

'Are you scared?'

'No.'

'So, let us in and you will know whether you are a criminal or not.'

He made way for them to enter and then closed the door.

The three men remained standing. He didn't ask them to sit.

'Can we sit?' asked an officer, all of them smiling. 'We are old people.'

'Yes, you can sit.' Now, he couldn't sip from his cup. Though he still held it, it was completely abandoned in his hands.

They took out a piece of paper with a rough hand written information on it. The officer looked at it a little and turned to Kennedy.

'Kennedy Foti is your name. Am I right?'

'Yes and why?' asked Kennedy still frowning with a bitter face and at this moment, his hand trembling.

'Hey young man, you just have to answer the questions. Is that right?'

Kennedy was silent.

'I have said you just need to answer the questions. Is that clear?' repeated the officer with more precisions. Kennedy was a little bit intimidated and forced to bow to that superior reaction.

'Thank you, Sir. Yes, Sir,' he fumbled.

'What do you do for a living?'

'Do you mean here in Germany?'

'Yes.'

'Nothing, Sir.'

The officer raised his head and looked at Kennedy. 'Do you have money in any bank?'

'Yes. MIB, Sir.'

'How did you get this money?'

'It was transferred from my account in my country to this new account.'

After all inquiries, they left.

* * * *

Dealers of any kind would account for any huge amount of money that would enter or leave any bank. In case of an unjustified source, when money entered the country, such an accounted was frozen.

MIB might have been shocked with the amount that came in. The law obliged the banks to declare to the police such a transaction for investigations.

Kennedy received proposal letters from two companies asking him to take shares, some months later. Kennedy contemplated for long on whether to accept share transfer or to buy a multimillion villa.

Seventeen

Foti continued to control the council.

One Friday early morning, the mayor leaned on a sofa at the waiting room answering a call. A man of about thirty years of age entered after a knock.

'Please,' said Foti, motioning his hand to the outside direction, 'wait there.' The man with a manila file humbled out. Then, Foti walked in to his own office after he dropped the call.

From his own office room, he dialled again and said, 'Sorry, someone obstructed me. We will talk later.'

It was 8 am. The secretary of council as she appeared to be wasn't there. The passageway that was a waiting room and a secretary's office was still empty. She was still to come. The mayor had created the post of secretary of council. Council laws didn't provide for such jobs in his municipality at that time. Foti was good in creating such jobs right from the time he was managing a first division football club.

'Please, can I help you? Come up to me. The secretary is not yet there.'

The man walked in fast.

'Good morning, Lord Mayor.'

'Good morning. How can I help you?'

'My name is Wilson Tah.' He stammered for several seconds and chocked mute. He had something to say but appeared shy.

'Are you ready to talk, Sir?'

'Yes, Sir,' responded Wilson. 'I have just heard that about five hundred private nurses will be absorbed by the government next month...'

'Yes,' interrupted Foti. 'You want integration, is that what you mean?'

'Yes, Sir. Yes, Sir... I want to...'

'Do you have the qualification?' he asked trying to make out which family bears the name Tah.

125

'You said you are Tah. Are you related to Tah Tebo popularly known as TT?'

'He is my father.'

'Oh, I see. He formed the *Njang dance* now sung on many occasions.'

'You are correct, Sir.'

'How did he compose such amazing songs and the unique ways of dancing? I know you were still very young then.' This time, the mayor was relaxed on his face.

'It was an inspiration from a song he heard.'

'Really? Where did he hear it?'

'When he once left for the Far North region to trade in cola nuts…'

'TT is dormant in politics. Is that?'

Wilson was quiet. He smiled. The mayor looked at him expecting something.

'Which party does he support, SDF?'

'No, Sir, he is of the CPDM.'

'Are you sure?'

'Yeah.'

'I have never heard of that, and you?'

'You know my father is getting too grey and isn't active enough.'

'And you, where do you lean?'

'I'm a member of the youth league (YL) of the ruling party.'

YL's main objective was to sensitise youths on democracy and the advantages of joining such a democratic party as CPDM.

Membership was free. All members were supposed to have small cards that identified and gave them the right to attend CPDM prayer meetings for free of charge.

'Do you have YL card?'

'I do Sir.' Wilson responded searching his pockets. He gave it to him. It was new. Upon the years, one of the conditions to fulfil if one wanted a government job was to be a member of the ruling party.

'… But it is just days old. Isn't it a ploy to convince me?'

'No, Sir. I had an old one but misplaced it.'

At this time, the secretary of council just entered the waiting room and a few people were desperately hovering there with files. The mayor could get the buzz from those waiting.

'Close that door,' he said to Wilson while studying the card. 'Where and for how long have you been practising?'

'I have been working at the Kobi private clinic for two years immediately after I completed from the Nursing Aid training.'

Foti swayed his head from side to side. Then he said, 'The government needs people with five years working experience to register them as state nurses. You know you lack some experience. You still need some time.'

Qualified candidates were supposed to compile documents and post them to the capital city for examination.

Wilson stood there still expecting the mayor to say something promising.

'Do you know you lack the qualification?' he repeated starring steadily at him.

'Please, just help me, Sir.'

'How do I help you? You aren't even an active member of the YL. When we advise people to sow where they can harvest, they don't seem to comply. These are the opportunities coming up for you to have a job.'

For a couple of seconds, no one spoke a word. However, the mayor portrayed a considerate face. His pen was on his lips, like he was thinking what to do.

'Do you know you are supposed to post your documents to Yaoundé?'

'I do, Sir.'

'Okay, I just want to help you.'

'Yes, Sir. Thank you, Sir. God bless you, Sir.'

The mayor raised his head to him with eyes wide open and asked, 'How much do you have?'

Wilson was desperate on his face. He was scraggy and unkempt. He scratched his hair and responded, 'I don't know, Sir. You can propose.'

'Do you have seven hundred?'

'I didn't get you, Sir.'

'I mean whether you have seven hundred thousand francs CFA.'

Wilson's lips shivered as he looked at the mayor. His biggest doubt was whether the Foti would accept half the amount proposed. There was another knock at the door. It was Lucy, the council secretary. She opened the door half way and said, 'There are many people here, Sir. They all want to see you.'

The mayor looked at her from her shoes, mini skirt and then to her eyes. 'You came almost an hour late today Lucy,' he said with friendly eyes. She didn't reply, but only thrust out her tongue and then closed the door.

'Tell them to exercise some patience,' he said in a huge voice that only reached her ears as echoes. He turned to Wilson.

'Say something, young man.'

'I have four hundred thousand francs, Sir.'

'No,' said the mayor closing the file. 'How much do I pay from here to Yaoundé? How much do I give them to consider you for the three years experience you lack?'

He didn't hand the file to Wilson immediately. He held it and looked at him convincingly. 'Do you have six hundred?'

'Five, Sir.'

For some five seconds, Foti was still contemplating. 'Is the five hundred handy?' he asked scratching his head.

'No. I will tell my uncle and we will come to see you tomorrow.'

'Are you sure?'

'Yes Sir.'

'I will keep your documents.'

'Alright, that is not a problem.'

They discussed everything and Wilson would meet the mayor the following day for handing over the amount accepted.

A man who had been in the waiting room entered. He had been there the previous day for civil status matters. As they discussed, the mayor's wife soon parked her car outside and walked in. 'Good morning,' she greeted those at the waiting room, walking straight into the office without looking at anyone's face. 'There is somebody in there, Madame,' said Lucy frowning.

'I know,' she replied. 'I have to rush to somewhere. I can't wait.'

She held a plastic shopping bag and a basket in both hands as she pushed the middle door with her right leg and entered.

'What again?' asked her husband.

'I just want to leave these things here. I will be back.'

'What is in the bag?'

'Some food items I have just bought.'

'Why not drop them at home first?'

'I told you that my uncle is leaving tomorrow for the States. I have to hand over what we bought for Jacky and Queen.'

'Ok. Sorry. It went off my mind. Extend my greetings. Maybe I will give him a call later on.'

His wife walked out. Her shoes were almost cracking the floor and the jingling of her bunch of car keys disturbing all ears. Lucy was not happy. 'Old useless woman,' she grumbled bitterly.

When she left, the mayor summarily attended to the man and then walked to the waiting room. He seemed tired.

'Hmmm, so many people here Lucy?' he said stretching himself.

At this time, Lucy was on her table cracking parched groundnuts from the shells and throwing them into her mouth one after the other. The people were waiting eagerly as three of them stood up wanting to go to him.

'Please be patient,' said the mayor. 'I will attend to all of you.'

He entered his office again and banged the door.

* * * *

That same day, medical volunteers were to address the local population of Tiko on HIV and AIDS and other diseases in front of the Tiko city hall. Mayor Foti would be there in the afternoon after which he would also address the councillors in the evening.

It was 2.30 pm. A group of seven medical officers were there. There were also about tens of nurses, university professors, and some other important guests. Professor Hansel was present at the occasion. A man many politicians considered insane because he wanted a perfect society, which was something impossible, as the people thought. Nevertheless, the professor kept on with his prayers on all the occasions he attended.

The mayor's wife sat amongst other most important women. Most of them were holding small handbags and car keys that jingled all the time. It was like a kind of pride to hold a bundle of car keys and be shaking them enjoyably. They were the women that mattered.

Five of the medical doctors, and a nurse lectured on AIDS. A barrister also gave his advice on awareness.

'We have lectured what we can,' said a leading doctor. 'We can't say everything. We now open room for anybody who has a contribution on how we can help combat HIV and AIDS and other diseases.

Abiga, the mayor's wife raised her hand. A man with a microphone rushed passed the crowd and handed it to her. She coughed timidly and said, 'In addition to what the learned Barrister has said about sensitisation, the authorities in charge should, and must knuckle on executing plans for sex education in schools. It has become a sing song on radio and television but nothing has ever been done...'

The doctor rose from his seat. 'Thank you, Madame,' he said. 'Everyone has a reason for a point proposed. I think that those concerned will do all at their disposal to execute the plans.'

A couple of hands were raised from the crowd. Most of the people at the back were standing. The seats were not enough. Professor Hansel was right in front. His hand too was up. The man with the microphone smartly and humbly rushed to him. His chubby and fallen jaws portrayed him as unsatisfied. It wasn't any doubt to those who knew him as a fighter for rights.

In a casual, though elegant attire, he gripped the microphone. He adjusted it several times while frowning and swaying his head from one side to the other.

'I am not a medical expert,' he said in a weak voice and people smiled and adjusted ready to listen. He returned the smile without any humour. 'It is a challenge for a collapsing society that the percentage of HIV positive victims is on a mad increase. It's like there will come a time that even non living things will have the infection.' People laughed. He coughed and continued. 'It puzzles me when medical experts lecture on ways of treating AIDS and consoling words to patients without mentioning of factors that cause this increase.'

People were more attentive at this time than before. Many people heaved forward to see Hansel.

'Really,' he continued, 'and secondly, I know HIV and AIDS kills. However, many other diseases like malaria, typhoid and others kill too if not more than AIDS.

The most important point I want to make here is poverty and corruption. These two are the major diseases that operate individually contributing to the increase of HIV and AIDS, making it greatest agony of our time. Believe me that if the thousands of young and unemployed graduates who have recruited themselves as prostitutes for almost no money are employed... AIDS patients will drop. Does an officer who employs an unqualified lady as secretary in his office, and later have unprotected sex with her, do any good to our society? Likely, he only passes it on, or carries the disease back home to meet his spouse. What sense does it make to spend huge sums to import contraceptives like condoms that the citizens are unable to afford or are not sensitised on how to use? Every day, we read the papers on how armed robbers rape during their operations. Do they use condoms during these devilish acts? No. This is even worse because there is a high probability that they will have blood contacts. You all know the story of one Eyong. He raped a sixteen-year-old girl, four months later, as the case was going on, the small girl was tested HIV positive. Medical doctors said and proved that Eyong passed it on to her. Two months later, while the case was pending for judgment, the defendant disappeared from custody. Until now that we are talking here, the police have been unable to give us an account of his whereabouts and how he escaped. I am sure that he bribed the police and ran away. By this time, he must have victimised other girls with the disease. People are just quiet and satisfied about it. Cameroon to me is a naive society. We seem to be so satisfied with many issues because we think that there is no way out, or we simply just fear to talk...'

When he stopped, the crowd applauded heavily.

* * * *

Later that evening, Mayor Foti presided over a council meeting. There was serious debate on issues like, allowances

132

for councillors, conditions for awarding contracts, assassination of the Mayor's character by some councillors and some other matters that arose.

At midnight, he was snoring heavily at the front side of the bed, while his wife Abiga was soothing his fat stomach.

As from the hour of twelve in the night, Tiko town was always almost dead. People were often afraid of the unholy men and the aggressive police officers. The only noise outside was that of crickets.

Foti heard some noise up the ceiling. It was like a dream. He held his breath and listened. There was nothing. He dumped his head again and within seconds, was vibrating like a steam engine. His body was broken from the much alcohol they had consumed before bed.

All windows of his mansion had quality protectors. It could be hard to get in through the window.

Some minutes later, just like he was in a nightmare this time, Foti heard something like a log of wood fell just near the bed. His heart bombed and he was awake. His eyes were open but the room was dark. He could see an unclear image near the door. He shook his wife.

'What is it?' she asked still with eyes closed.

'It is like there is someone standing there near the door,' he whispered in response. She raised her head but couldn't make any difference. Her head fell back on the pillow. Foti climbed down and switched on the light. A man of enormous muscles was standing there starring at them. Foti trembled terribly and his voice just dried off.

'Ssssp,' hissed the man with his index finger on his lips. Abiga woke and was on her senses then. She sobbed. The man fired at the wall. 'If you shout, I will shoot at you. Cover that large mouth, you dirty woman.'

The man was dressed in a black shirt over a black trouser. He covered his whole head with a hair scarf with only two tiny holes for him to see.

At the beginning of that confusion, they heard a huge slap from the next room, a terrible spank on Harrison's jaw, as he cried out.

The man in black opened the door to Foti's parlour. In there was two sets of ostentatious caution chairs at a corner, a plasma TV, a glass cupboard with various glasses, cups, spoons, luxurious wine and spirit bottles, and many others. Some of them seemed never used even once but seemed to have been there for long.

Two other men entered with pistols and appeared lethal. They aggressively tugged Foti and his wife to the sitting room. From the other rooms, they also dragged Harrison and an aunt that was there for a visit into the sitting room and asked them to lie flat silently on the floor.

One of the strange people stood at the front door, the other at the back door, and one other was watching the other three people in action. They were a dangerous crew of six inside. It was obvious that there were some more outside.

The man near the front side of the door sent his hand outside through the window and took a packet of cigarette. They were all dressed the same way. For about two minutes, three of them were sucking from their cigarettes and pumping out smoke to the ceiling. One stood pointing a gun at them with his leg on the hips of Abiga. The other two robbers were in a serious and brutal search- in briefcases, wardrobes, in suits, boxes and cupboards.

For about three minutes of searching, they found nothing. They gave four kicks on the hips of Abiga and one of them asked, 'Do you want us to ask before you show the money?' Another robber walked to Foti and placed his knee on his spinal cord while dragging fast from his cigarette to finish it. Foti cried in a tiny voice.

'Close your stinky mouth, idiot,' shushed the man. 'I have not even touched you.'

He dropped the cigarette and turned to Foti. 'We need money,' he said. 'Where is it? Tell us fast.'

The mayor's voice dried off again. He only motioned his trembling hand to the direction of the room. He gave him two heavy blows and asked, 'Don't you want to talk?'

Again, he gripped him from his thick *swine neck* and pulled him back to the room. The other two robbers remained in searching. He hit him in a horrifying way and one of his two artificial teeth fell off his mouth. Blood oozed. He began to shake like one in high fever and didn't want to lose another tooth. He pointed to a small television. 'There,' he said.

'Here how?' asked the man turning the small television up and down. No money was seen. Another robber walked to him and placed a pistol on his lips. 'If you waste our precious time, we will waste your useless life. Have you heard me? Take the money and give us faster,' he said adjusting the pistol in his hand. Before the mayor could nod his head in acceptance, he held him from the neck and threw him like a useless article to the wall. Foti dangled and the robber immediately picked him again from the jaws with two hands like a wrestler. He was ready to show where the money was. He said, 'It is inside the TV, Sir. I will open it for you.'

Foti was somehow wise. He put the money in a small old TV because no thief could care to steal such an outdated thing. When he unscrewed the television and huge bundles came from it, none of them could believe what they saw. They continued to force him and he brought down another bundle from the ceiling in the room. They pulled him to the sitting room again.

Abiga was stripped naked. A man turned her flat with no least sorrow, pushed her legs sideways and climbed on her, blocking her mouth with his face. Then, he did it brutally. She was dying under that weight. She was empty of dignity, hope, and of the entire life.

The man got up. Foti's face was to that direction but he held his breath and closed his eyes tightly. A second man pulled down his trousers halfway and climbed on her. 'Please,' she cried, 'I will die if you continue.'

'Your death is my portion,' responded the man forcing his thing into her. Her hands were open and pressed to the ground even though she could do nothing if allowed to react.

Another man was on Foti's aunt seriously moving his body up and down.

Foti could not open his eyes to see the filthy drama. One of them slapped him and asked him to open his eyes to watch the game. '*Just fuckam small small. No killam,*' said another with some sympathy.

The carpet became red. The victims were swimming in their own pool of blood but the robbers did not care. Outside, two men were standing near a bus without a number plate. They all held guns and knives attached to their belts.

Before leaving, they cut off the house telephone, and seized three handsets. The last person to leave keyed both doors and threw the keys far away into darkness. They edged the bus to the narrow road and disappeared.

Foti waited for a few minutes and walked breathlessly to the window. He was still to gain full sight after the many blows and slaps on his face.

He resuscitated his broken wife and aunt to the room and helped dressed them up.

The unidentified gunmen were gone. Until this time, he didn't realise that they left with one of his luxurious cars. When he stepped out at 6 am, he couldn't fine it. He informed his neighbours and they came out in their numbers to share the grief.

Mayor Foti wasn't too worried about the money, nor the car taken away. His main worry was the abuses on his wife and aunt. In addition, he couldn't imagine such beatings on him and he thought also that such web of activity could repeat itself.

At this time in Tiko and the entire national territory, such acts were at an increase following the rise in economic austerity.

It was risky walking late in the night because men of a different world owned it. Such hazardous nights were becoming severe because of blackouts.

Foti's face was deformed. He couldn't say anything about his car. He entered the house leaving the people out with hands on their jaws. He said to Harrison, 'Never tell anybody what happened. Have you understood?'

'Yes, Dad.'

'Don't even say you witnessed the scene. If asked, say you were in your room. Is that right?'

He carried his hands on his head still trying to imagine what bad luck befell him. 'This is an abomination,' he exclaimed in his throat. 'Death is better than to witness this kind of a thing. This is a ridiculous thing that is tarnishing to my image as mayor of this town. I will die, oh my God! I will die!'

A neighbour explained that he heard some strange noise on the streets and later, it was coming from the mayor's compound. The man said he tried to reach the mayor on his mobile but to no success and that he later tried the police office but it rang for long and nobody took the phone. So, he dropped and fell asleep.

When he entered his room, Abiga was beating herself on the bed from back to front, and weeping in a tiny voice.

'Darling,' he said soothing her hair, 'I have to rush two of you to the hospital. I have told those people outside that they only brutalised us. You should not let anybody know that this happened. Don't also let them know that they left with a huge sum of money.'

In front of the mayor's residence, neighbours watched the broken Abiga and mayor's aunt helped into the car. As they stood talking to each other, a daily breakfast bread supplier to the mayor's home came with words. He said an unidentified gunman shot a secondary school teacher dead that same night. People were overwhelmed.

Sooner, they were at the Tiko hospital. Such rape cases needed something more than normal medical attention. Experts with technical psychological ministration would be so indispensable.

* * * *

At 8 am, when offices were resuming, security officers and gendarmes were in serious control. It seemed late. The men were gone for good.

The death of a secondary school teacher raised serious alarm for security officers and politicians.

At mid day, human right activists, lawyers, teachers and others, joined the National Chair for the opposition party to address the issue.

The murdered teacher, Tita Tendong from the Northwest region wasn't only a secondary school teacher; he was also a man of extreme dynamism. His Sunday afternoon program, *Reaching the Youths* with the Southwest regional Radio station, was gaining prominence. Because of it, youths were able to talk to great men about their successes, how they too could excel. The show helped direct the youths and it also curbed emigration by about two percent. It helped to explain to the youths that they needed to stay and fight for the future of their fatherland than fly out to the west.

On the streets of Tiko, many people would call him *Father of All Children*. Unfortunately, he didn't enjoy these titles for long. That bad Friday morning, a taxi driver, at about 5.30 am discovered his body. Someone had shot him on the chest and his throat cut deep.

When Foti and the abused family reached the hospital, from a distance, they could see a group of people wailing. Some others were crawling on the ground. The

National Chair for SDF gave an impromptu visit to Tiko that morning.

As Nde Fed stood to address the people, lawyers also stood there to express their legal minds. They were ready to drag the police, gendarmes and the state to court for insecurity.

Fed coiled his face and shook his head. 'We are a society that hates itself,' he said. His eyes dimmed and tears dripped. Many people that heard him from a distance on the microphone began approaching. 'We hate ourselves,' he repeated. 'We hate development.' He turned his head as he choked with anger. 'Professor Hansel once said,' he quoted, 'our society is meandering into a passageway of demise and that once our society passes that bridge, we cannot bring it back.' When we make speeches, papers describe them as pre-election gambits. What excuse can the police give for not answering a call in the night? Were they on night duties or on sleep duties?'

People forced out smiles. He continued, 'There in the hospital mortuary is a man who was helping to open the eyes of the youths thereby shaping the country for a better tomorrow. Well, the regime in power also tastes the bitterness of the kind of society they are constructing. We spend all our precious time watching fatal scenes and making speeches. Still, the same things repeat themselves and even more worse.

Just yesterday, we were singing on AIDS. Today, we are here. When shall we build and enjoy our society? Who are those going to build this society? The youths, who are not given the chance? Or the great minds who are assassinated daily?'

Fed stepped aside. The bâtonnier for Southwest region heaved from the growing crowd.

'We are not going to put hands on jaws. We want to fight again and this time, even more. This is a total challenge. We are not going to go after those on the run for now. We have to start with the regime in power and those security officers who have turned station offices into sleeping rooms, if only they were even there in the night. Tomorrow might be your own day to face an attack. So, please join us in this fight. The government and the police will have to explain this to us in a court of law. We extend our heartfelt condolence to the bereaved family. Thank you.'

The group of lawyers walked away. They would meet again next day for an emergency meeting. They were ready to do it.

Eighteen

Foti, his wife and aunt recovered. Just two weeks after hospital, Abiga left for the States to meet her daughters.

At this time, Foti was drinking just a bottle of beer, or a glass of spirit, than the many bottles he used to empty. Perhaps, this was because of his loneliness. It was a numbing period for the mayor. He would put on a good face on the streets and on occasions but back at home, Foti was sad.

At 4 pm on Monday, Lucy keyed Foti's office and walked behind him to the road. She entered the car and they drove off to his home.

That evening, Lucy assisted Foti. She prepared his dresses for next day and cooked for him. They ate together, drank beer and watched television. It was the first day Lucy ever felt relaxed beside the financial wizard. She wished such days were more and longer.

She sipped from a beer glass as if she was sipping hot tea. Then she looked at Foti. He carried his hand to her verdant front side. 'You are just such a sweet lady,' he said. She breathed comfortably and smiled. 'Thank you,' she replied carrying her leg to his. 'Such moments do not last long,' she added.

'What do you mean?'

'Your wife will be back soon and my time will be off.'

'She will be long there. We have all the time.'

Foti leaned backwards on the chair and she was there on his heavy tummy soothing it but he was soon snoring heavily. She woke him and they walked to the bedroom.

Later on in the night, she carried on the duties of Abiga with much courtesy. To her, it was a night to remember.

* * * *

At 5 am the followin1g day, Lucy woke him from a deep sleep. She gave him the best that early morning before preparing him for the journey.

Foti had four files to take to the capital city, including that of Wilson Tah. For two weeks, Wilson had been praying for Foti's quick recovery. It wasn't for any compassion but for the wish to be a state registered nurse.

It was obvious that the number of places were distributed evenly according the ten regions of the country.

In the afternoon, Foti arrived. Outside the ministry of public health, he met other public figures with files. He was almost late. He ascended to the second floor of the building and entered a room. A man sat there seriously making stamps on files and a lady checking them one after the other.

As Foti entered, from the door, the man could recognise him.

'Lord Mayor,' said the man warmly.

'Yes, Chief.'

'Look at your watch,' he said so pointing to his wrist and shaking his head, though with a smile. 'Africans are Africans,' he added.

'Accept my apology. You can imagine the bad roads and the many traffic jambs.'

'Mr. Foti, I could not keep waiting. I have only two places reserved for you, instead of five.'

Foti was astonished. He opened his eyes and his mouth was ajar. 'I am finished,' he cried out. 'Please don't do this to me. I have assured the people.'

Foti took two glasses of water as if he had been thirsty for days. He sat and opened a file, licking his index finger and crosschecking them. The Chief looked at them and said, 'You have to understand, Mr. Foti. Those who have sent in their documents are qualified. If I have to replace some of them with your candidates, it should not be a matter of many. It is your fault, you have come late.'

'Chief,' he pleaded further, 'this is business. These candidates have been participating in our party activities. In addition, I have something to encourage your efforts. You have your cola nut, Chief.'

Foti was frantic on his face. As the man explained, he was rushing over about five thousand files.

After the long argument, Foti Was left with no option than to submit the files of two of his candidates. They began dragging the amount.

'So, how much do I give for a file?' asked Foti. The Chief raised his head adjusting his glasses with his left index finger from the bridge.

'I have noticed you for one thing, Mr. Foti.'

'What is that?'

'Are you new? You know how much you have to offer.'

'This time, I have six hundred for the two files.' The Chief felt hurt. 'I hope it is not a provocation.' He frowned and didn't wait for Foti to say a word. 'Last time you pleaded for nine hundred for two files and I considered you.'

'Those were candidates for magistracy,' interrupted Foti. 'That is something big, Sir. Do you want me to fuel your car with the same amount when it is a low job? Honestly speaking, they didn't give me a single franc for the files. I want to help them just for the fact that they are members of the Youth League of our party.'

Anger was wailing on the Chief's face. Foti tried to argue further.

'You like to dilly-dally,' said the Chief.

'What do you mean by that?'

'You like to bid prices even on priceless things.'

Foti was still swaying his head in a respectful way of disagreement. 'Even at the presence of a beautiful lady like this,' added the man laughing, 'you are still penny-pinching.'

The lady smiled and said, 'The title *Lord Mayor* should also be respected and appreciated by the bearer.'

'I know,' he said. 'But it doesn't mean I should creep on mud for that.'

'I mean you deep your hands into the pocket with dignity. Come on man!'

'You women can make a piece of fertile land go deserted as well as create a body of water in the desert.'

Though Foti said so, the lady's tender and appealing voice emasculated him. He took out a coffee brown envelope from his briefcase, handed the amount to him, and looked at the lady. 'I hope I have acted as a mayor?'

'No. You have just acted as a young man begging for a job.' They all laughed. At this time, the lady's voice and smiles charmed Foti. He gave the lady some few notes.

Foti was about to leave. 'I hope we meet again,' he said.

'So, how are you pulling on with your zone?' asked the Chief as Foti stood to leave.

'I am doing my utmost best to clean all the dirt. We are sure for a landslide in next elections.'

'Watch out for espionage. It's very important.'

'Yeah, you are right. We have set a secret group of experts to take care of spy. They have already identified two opposition party cowards who were out for our plans to maintain the council. We proved them of their deceitful minds, and immediately, we expelled them. There is another spy. He is so strong in his defence, but we are twisting the case to corruption charges on him…'

'Oh yes. I remember the millions of fiscal stamps that were missing.'

'Yes.'

'But your members were involved in that deal.'

'Hmmm…, yes but we have to fight for their exoneration in all ways. After that, we cap everything on him.'

'No. If you people can fight him quit the party, let him go with the crime.'

'There is one thing you must know. Information reaching us from the central secretariat is that there are plans for a coalition among the SDF and those three mushroom groups. Who knows what happens if a coalition works out?'

'What has the coalition got to do? If you combine all the small parties, it will still make no sense. It does not make up to fifty percent in the parliament for them to challenge our bills.

'No, Chief. Some people might change their minds if they find an increase in that direction. If there is a way to deal away with the strong people even to their deaths, it would be much more preferable. We just simply have to prevent it than wait to cure any such disaster.'

The lady had been putting stamps on some files. She snitched and said, 'I heard something about the coalition.'

'What is that?'

'That it has been secretly formed but a problem arose. The Chair for each of the parties wants to be the coalition candidate. Each one of them insists on ruling if they are successful. That is how the idea of a coalition failed.'

'Oh yes,' interrupted Foti. 'I can understand. You know Christopher Naye, Chair for Christian Democrats, is a lawyer. You know lawyers claim they know everything meanwhile they are trained liars. I think he must have spoiled the idea.'

For sure, Foti hated anything in the name of a lawyer. Lawyers often challenged him in court. It was due to the strength of his money that he went with most of his crimes.

He left but was not too happy. Only two of his files were treated.

* * * *

For over the months, news was spreading that a group of most successful politicians around the world would award any African leader who helped fight bribery and corruption, give writers and journalists the rights they deserve, and to allow international press cover events in their various countries where necessary. At the same time, the group would identify and expose corrupt governments for sanctions.

It was for this reason that the government set a secret commission to sort out files of corrupt officers and to forward them to the headquarters for thorough examination.

A state was not only going to have the awards. Its leader could possibly benefit from crime exoneration, debt cancellation, scholarships given to students, construction work and many others.

Many leaders didn't do it for that reason but for fears of being identified and possibly arrested. At this time, the world was watching former Liberian president tormented at The Hague, and the Sudanese leader in panic of arrest. At this time also, the western boys were holding and pulling the legs of the Zimbabwean leader. Unfortunately, at this time, he was fighting hard to stay in power.

The government secret commission was out, in various regions of the country, seriously searching for corrupt persons. This was another problem for Foti.

Nineteen

Three private journalists were under arrest. Amongst them was Akuro Ngam, a long time friend to late Tanga. They arrested him for having published articles criticising the electoral commission. He was a member of an international human rights organisation, Freedom International. Its main objective was to send pressure appeals to governments to release political detainees who were not guilty of any crime.

Ngam's absence from the streets raised an international outrage. He was a human right activist and a journalist.

Appeals were coming in from countries around the world. It all made no difference. For that reason, NI's journalist Stella Woods set in for investigation. NI was News International.

At ten o'clock in the morning, Stella stood at the gate of maximum-security prison at the capital city, accompanied by a camera operator. She rang several times but no officer came out. As they stood there waiting, a police officer was passing just close to them. Stella approached him.

'Good morning, Sir.'

'Morning, can I help you?'

'Yes, Sir. I am a journalist.'

'Yes, I know. You are Stella from NI.'

'Yeah, that's interesting. Do you watch NI?'

'Daily.'

'That is so interesting to hear. Is this the maximum security prison of the capital city?'

'Yes. What is the problem?'

'I want to get in. We have permission and a rendezvous with a journalist detained here.'

As they spoke, a guard came round from the back and spoke with her. At first, the guards refused her from entering.

She presented all necessary documents and they made many calls before she was accepted.

For over decades, no journalist ever stepped legs into the maximum-security prison. No human rights group has ever done so too.

When a guard told Ngam that NI was to talk to him at a waiting room, he thought they wanted to take him to a final minute. He could think only of death, but that wasn't the case.

There in prison, he was always with a pant and slippers given to him as prison dresses. This time, before he met Stella, he was dressed in a shirt, a trouser and a pair of sandals. They all smelled as dresses kept in a cold place and unclean for several months.

The guard puttered along a passageway. Ngam followed hopelessly from behind. Stella had been waiting for about forty-five minutes. A NI camera operator stood near the door ready to cover the event. The guard was making sure not to appear on the camera.

At first, Stella didn't have the courage to talk to Ngam. Sometimes, journalists make some kind of research on the person concerned before interview. Stella must have done it from the first question she asked him.

'I am Stella, a NI journalist. Are your Ngam Akuro?'

'Yes,' he replied nodding his head repeatedly.

'I mean the detained journalist.'

'Yes, Madame.'

Perhaps, she couldn't believe he was the person she saw on the internet. He was a man of about eighty kilograms but had lost about half of it. He was weary, skinny and appeared to die soon if the situation persisted.

She didn't ask him if he was feeling good in health. Rather, she asked, 'Do you receive medication for your ill health?'

'Don't ask that question,' he responded after several seconds trying to gather some energy. He coughed and added, 'You don't have to ask whether a monkey shot by a hungry hunter would be rushed for resuscitation. They have been searching for pretexts to trap people like us and kill through maltreatment. How can one talk of medication?'

'If this continues, it is categorically clear that you will die.'

'Sure,' he interrupted, 'I will die. That doesn't matter. I think that the spirits of those who die this way only go to reshape the road to justice. Let our administrators and the forces of law and order be informed that either in this world or in the world beyond, they shall account for all they do.'

'What were your reactions to Tanga's death?'

'I miss him. He remains a legend in memory. It is not just that I lost a colleague, but that the nation and the entire world lost a great and committed journalist. He was an indispensable force in this field. The reactions of all journalists, I in particular was an appeal for a thorough investigation into his death and to bring those involved to justice.'

'What was the result?'

'Until this moment, the government reports that the investigations are going on. If up to this moment there are no results, I think there shall never be. I think one cannot ask soldiers in jubilation whether they are responsible for the deaths of rival soldiers in battle. However, I am appealing to all journalists, writers, and reporters to form a unique international body for a stronger safeguard.'

'A few countries around the world have this kind of body you are talking about operating for many years now, though not an international body. Is your country having a national association for journalists?'

'Unfortunately, the answer is no. Only writers do have a zombie association. We have been falling prey to the forces of law and other. That is why I am appealing for something international.'

'What are the difficulties faced in forming a body?'

'This is a country with about two hundred and fifty ethnic groups with about two hundred and seventy indigenous languages and different cultures. It is also a bilingual country with a bi-jural system of law. This stemmed from a joined colonial rule. So it makes it difficult for us to stand in one voice, though we are struggling towards that direction.'

'I have read briefly about this,' she interrupted. 'How does it affect journalists and writers who want to form an association?'

'Yes, I was about coming to that point.'

'We are regionalists and no matter how fruitful an idea is, a man from another tribe would not want to share. A French speaking man would not want to bow to an English-speaking boss, and vice versa. It is the same amongst journalists and writers. This poor way of reasoning has transcended to political parties. The western powers that caused this confusion on our continent are enjoying harmony, while we continue in the mess.'

'Do you sympathise with any political party?'

'Not really. I, hmmm, hmmm,' he stammered. Stella put the question again closing her file as if the questions were exhausted. 'I mean whether you belong to any political group.'

'The answer is no. I am disappointed with both the political system and the various parties we have. I only share positive political ideas, those that can change our nation and the world. I share in true democracy and justice, irrespective of which party exercises it.'

'Sorry to interrupt. Like late Tanga, the government has accused you of secessionist ideologies, reading news that could lead to violence, abusing and condemning the electoral commission as government controlled, this means you seem to be a sympathiser to the opposition party. Aren't you?'

'No, though they might think so. It is clear that Tanga supported the SDF. I am neutral in politics. I have been emphasising on dirty acts by both the opposition and ruling parties.'

'Have you ever condemned the electoral commission?'

'Yes. The whole thing has a base on a hideous text, and they don't like it to face any challenge or castigation from any citizen. My criticisms didn't come in because it concerns the ruling party. Whether of the ruling party or opposition, I would like to criticize any unjust action. There is clear injustice. '

'Give an example.'

'Imagine that top officials of the commission are staunch militants of the ruling party that resigned from the party. The commission is supposed to be independent. The government is simply cooking a time bomb and I believe it will explode one day, a kind of thing I personally don't want to happen in this society. Honestly speaking, I hunger for peace in my country because I know what it means going to war. I love a society with perfect tranquillity.'

'What activities of the opposition have you ever criticised?'

'I wrote lengthily about the SDF Chair. When a coalition formed amongst opposition parties, he insisted that if they do succeed, he would take the lead. He gave his reason that his party carries the majority amongst the opposition parties. When he received opposition to that, he stepped aside from the coalition and that is why it has just collapsed. You can see from that uncivilized way that there is no democracy even amongst those who want to grab and control power.'

'Does Obama mean anything to you? Or, what do you expect from the US president?'

'He seems to be a powerful man emerging so strongly in the realm of politics. His coming to power has changed the mentality of people around the world. His *Yes We Can* speech is evocative to many young people around the globe. I also do appreciate his courage and commitments to making peace. I do expect a lot of empathy from him on trade.'

'What aspect? Do you mean financial support?'

'Far from that. I expect him to lobby for honest trade between Africa and the western world. Trade or relationships between Africa and the west should not be exploitative and cruel as is the case today. African leaders are being manipulated.'

'Can you identify and expatiate on any aspect of cruelty?'

'Look, there are many wars and hunger on this fertile and blessed continent. I would like to quote you an example here.'

'Go on.'

'You get gold and diamond and supply me with weapons at a cheaper price that I can fight the opposition and remain in power. If you help me remain in power, I will always supply our petrol and timber only to you... From where do you think African warriors get their weapons? Do you think they manufacture them? No. Just imagine that at the time political turmoil was going on in Zimbabwe, a Chinese ship carrying war weapons was labouring towards South African waters. It was after a long time and after heavy reports that the ship had to return. They are a kind of exchanging weapons and their financial support to African leaders for mineral resources. New reports coming in now from CNN say war weapons in Sudan have been reported being imported from China. China has backed it up saying they are trading in weapons legally with Sudan...'

'Will you continue to write and report if you are released from detention?'

'I believe writing and reporting is a gift. It is a call and if I am behind bars because of my writing, I think that my pen is making a big difference. That should be the more reason for me to go on writing. It means it is having an effect.

It means it is helping to transform our collapsing society. Even if I should die, physical death is not the worst thing that can happen to a man. It is spiritual death. But I have submitted my will into the will of God.'

'It was nice talking to you.'

'Thank you for having me.'

When she left, the guard held Ngam along the passageway and pushed him into his small room.

Twenty

One morning, two weeks after Foti was back from the capital city, at the pace of a snail, he drove to his office. It seemed something wasn't going on well.

At the same time he sat in his office thinking about what would happen Wilson entered to ask if he succeeded in processing his documents. He explained to him why he could not make it. He couldn't refund his money but promised him that he would use it to make him succeed an examination into a police college.

His office radio was on, and he was ready to get the news before getting into files. Before news headlines from the radio, Kingsley knocked at the door. At normal and happy moments, Kingsley would say in a loud voice, 'The Lord Mayor.' But that morning, it wasn't the case. He knocked and entered the office without saying a word. Even when news used to be bad, he had never been that sad. Foti looked at him expecting him to deliver the bad news.

He threw himself on the chair and folded his arms, but holding a newspaper.

'Have you read *The Watch Newspaper* this morning?'

'No,' he responded with raised head. 'What is in the making?'

He threw the newspaper on the table without saying a word. Foti picked it up and looked at the front page. One of the main headlines was *A Man Claims Responsibility for the Death of Tanga.*

He didn't continue reading but looked at his friend with surprise. At the length of about two minutes, both men were silent. For Foti, it was a bolt from the blue. After several seconds, Kingsley said, 'We have fought wars, but for this one, we have to retreat.'

It was clear that if Achiri confessed that they killed Tanga in a hotel room, he could possibly say the names of the

155

master planners. That was their doubt and confusion. The frustration began.

They closed themselves in the office making confused proposals and rejecting it at the same time. There was clear uncertainty.

After about thirty minutes, Lucy was at the waiting room with a contractor who wanted to talk with the mayor.

Foti didn't want to talk any business that morning. Lucy knocked, opened and informed him that someone was there waiting. 'Tell any person who is there and any other that comes that we don't work today. Let them come some other time,' Foti said.

The man could hear him talking to Lucy. When she walked back to her seat, Foti keyed the door. He was never the type who could give up easily. He remained at the same spot cracking out his mind for a solution.

'He is in detention in Yaoundé,' he said. Foti supported his head with his hand as he thought further.

'What do you think, Foti?' Without any waste of time, he responded to his own question, 'We have to take action. Let us kill him there immediately.'

'How can that work?' Foti asked and breathed out heavily. He thought for about five seconds. 'We need to pay somebody to poison him there. That is the only way now. You know people are heavily starved there.'

'We have to wait for a few days and see what happens to him next before taking action.'

'No, Kingsley,' he laughs perfunctorily. 'We don't give him room to leak all secrets.'

As the minutes were ticking off, fear was mounting in them. The two fat cats feared surprises and decided to leave for Kingsley's. His wife was at the job side while his four children were in school.

At one o'clock that afternoon, at Kingsley's, Foti's mobile telephone rang. He clicked it to answer but in that

156

fumbling, he had no time to look at the screen. He simply said, 'I am busy please.'

'Who was that?' asked Kingsley.

'I didn't look.'

'This is the time to be more careful. You have to know any call that comes in and why.'

He picked his mobile and looked at *received calls*. It was the Tiko police calling.

'Hey, your boys have called.'

It rang again. He picked it up. One of the police officers told him that an unknown group of eight just asked for help on how to get to the Tiko council. They equally told Foti that the people were suspicious.

Several minutes later, as they sat contemplating, they saw a strange car negotiating a corner towards Kingsley's home. He walked to the window and watched keenly.

Foti was quick to understand the situation. Swiftly and through the back door, the mayor was on escape leaving behind his car.

One of the officers greeted Kingsley warmly. Before he could realise, two others suddenly fell in and surrendered him with a 12-guage gun.

'You are under arrest,' said one of them. They presented an arrest warrant and introduced who they were. 'We have to drive you to the Buea awaiting trial prison for questioning. We are arresting you because you are presumed to be involved in the death of one Tanga.'

He wanted to argue. 'You don't need to argue. It is simply an allegation. You will have the chance to prove your innocence.'

They shoved the bundled commissioner into the car and drove off. They had no knowledge of the mayor's escape through the back door. He had slid into a nearby bush. The arrest of the commissioner and disappearance of Foti raised many questions.

* * * *

Early in the morning, Lucy tiptoed to the mayor's house and collected his passport. Outside the house just at the door, two men surrendered her with a pistol. 'Don't move and don't shout,' said a man going closer to her. Two other officers emerged from the flowers. She identified herself in big panic. The words 'I am secretary of council' didn't please them. They arrested and searched her.

It was shocking that they saw his passport and national identity card in her bag. It was clear she knew the mayor's whereabouts, but she claimed she didn't. There wasn't any doubt. She was declared a suspect and taken away.

On the third day, after the escape, the papers were making huge sums of money from sales. First in a lifetime, the ruling party godfathers wrote, 'We must find the murderers.'

Cartoon newspapers were also sketching more than ever. In the night, an unidentified cartoon artist painted a captivating image on the council wall: a man with heavy jaws, big belly and tiny legs, a gun and huge sums of money was dropping from the hands of the caricature, and police officers were pursuing him with dogs. Beside the ugly image, the cartoon artist wrote, 'The mayor on escape.'

After the official announcement of Foti's escape, a few other people did disappear.

Twenty-One

Kennedy was too worried about the whereabouts of his father. He couldn't get his father on the phone for several days and feared he was caught.

His father was agile, courageous, and active and was very fast to react. For several days, the police couldn't find him. Before his photo was handed to all border police, the Nigerian border police identified it and reported that they saw a man of that description enter Nigeria. They also said they questioned him, and he backed up himself with documents as a motor spare part trader.

He was making serious progress. Two days later, he called his son from Lagos International Airport. He was about to take off but his son was not happy on the phone. 'Is it so serious that you can't fight it and stay home? If you leave the country now, your political chapter is closed and you will be hunted daily.'

He responded, 'Politics is an actor and audience game. I was a good actor and my series has ended. I just want to join the audience and watch others on the stage. You don't have to bother. I have rewarded myself and from it, I will hugely live.'

* * * *

At ten that night, he took off and some hours later, he was approaching European soils. What was left of his golden eggs was simple regurgitation.

It was gradually dawning to another day. With great and known punctuality, Lufthansa landed at the Düsseldorf International Airport at 6 am.

At the exit, Foti was heavily questioned. His face was huge, but the photo on his passport showed that he had a thin face. It was an old passport and was hard to prove many features on it.

'Where were you born, mister?' asked a police officer.

'In Lagos,' responded Foti. Many other questions followed: his place of birth, how many visas he had on his passport and where it was issued. He answered all questions correctly but they were still not convinced. He became too nervous and spoke in hard words to the officers.

'Sir, we doubt you and your passport. We have to take down your fingerprints and then allow you go. Is that alright, Sir?'

'Am I a suspect?'

'No. We do this whenever there is a doubt.'

'What the hell are you telling me? That a man should not eat and grow fat because of fears that German police would question him?' The police didn't bother. They allowed him to bubble and settle. When he calmed down, they took his fingerprints and a photocopy of his passport and allowed him go. He was not himself.

Foti was a man whose footsteps used to compose a story of great ambiance and achievement. This time, he walked away with miserable and unpromising steps.

Kennedy had been waiting to receive him for about an hour. He didn't doubt much what could have delayed him at the exit.

From a distance, after some length of time, Foti appeared from between the arriving crowd and his doldrums was expressed from the way he walked. When he received his father, Kennedy said, 'God being so kind.'

They drove off from the airport. His desolation didn't move his son the least but he was thinking heavily to himself. Kennedy had always been a stoic character, and most of his responses were always affirmative in benefit of a peaceful life. His fiancée had always quarrelled with him for such a passive attitude. She was tired of it and their relationship seemed to be spacing out more and more.

* * * *

A short time ago, Kennedy had been convinced to accept a ten percent share transfer in a company producing pain killer drugs. That cost about three quarters of his total money.

Although he doubted how companies knew he could be capable of taking up such a big business, he didn't seek his father's advice or that of any legal adviser.

Before he undertook to sign for share transfer, a group of people were dragging the company, PainKi, to court. They claimed that the company didn't warn that the drug could lead to paralyses if overdosed. The claim was millions of Euros, but Kennedy was never told this. At the same time, the company though it would decline responsibility.

* * * *

At arrival at home, father and son took their breakfast and sat discussing the dilemma.

'You see why I have always said it is good to be sharp and agile,' said Foti. 'Just imagine them arresting and throwing me into jail.' He boxed on the sofa and said, 'God forbid, not Foti.'

For all this while, his son was silent. 'You are silent, Ken, nothing to offer?'

'I am just thinking about it, Dad.'

'Look, you have to change. If you were in my position, you would have been arrested.'

After several minutes, he told his father, 'The only solution now is for you to seek asylum in Switzerland and try to withdraw the money from BIB.'

Foti scratched his head in a mode of deepest frustration. He sighed and looked up to the sky through the window, as was his habit. He yawned and said nothing.

'Or you don't think so, Dad?'

'You are right. Very right, but with what documents Am I going to ask for part of this money?'

'You think you will lose this vast sum? No.'

'I won't, but you have to know that it is fifty on fifty. It's more complicated without documents. Up to this moment, the frozen assets of Mobutu still hang there.'

'You will have to seek asylum with your real names and if granted, you will be able to use your documents to clear the sum. Simple.'

'I know. It is possible. The only obstacle is that my fingerprints were taken and attached to the passport I used.' This was confusing to Kennedy. He knew a little about asylum procedure and thought it could be complicated. At this time, Kennedy ignored three calls even without looking at the screen to know who was calling. A fourth call came two minutes later. He asked his son to pick it up. 'It's from the US,' he sad.

'Dad has arrived successfully. We will call you back in a tick. Is that ok with you?' He immediately dropped the phone and looked at his father. Foti thought even if things became worst, he could still make life from the investment he made on his son.

'How much interest do you make in a month, Ken?'

'What do you mean?'

'How are you consolidating your financial stand?'

Kennedy didn't say a word.

'I hope that stillness is not expressing a problem. Is there any trouble?'

'Not really. I now hold shares in a company, PainKi.'

'What was your assessment before engaging into the deal? Who advised you on that?' He maintained silence for a second time.

'Did you contact any business consultant or any legal personnel?'

'Not really.'

'This is not home. This is a different world, Ken...
What does Pain... what was the name again?'

'PainKi.'

'What does it deal in?'

'From its appellation, it simply deals in pain killer
drugs.'

'How many percent shares?'

Ken stammered and responded in a low voice, 'Ten
percent. About three quarters of what I had has been used for
the deal.' Foti's bones dislodged. He was jittery. He rose from
his seat speechless and walked to the window, then turned
and looked at Kennedy whose head was supported with both
hands.

'Do you know what you have done, Ken?'

He didn't want to say a word. Rather he took a cube
of sugar from a packet and licked it casually. His father made
way between the sofas into the toilet. For fifteen minutes, he
didn't hear from him. The toilet was half way open. Kennedy
tiptoed and watched. His father was sitting on the toilet with
his head buried in his knees. At first sight, he thought he had
collapsed.

'Dad,' he called shaking him. Foti fumbled and was
immediately awake. 'Where am I? Oh, God... I didn't sleep
on board.'

He left him there to dress up. When he left for the
sitting room, Ken said, 'I know I have made a mistake. I
thought it was just a way to make money grow rather than sit
at home and get stagnant.'

'Yes, you are very right,' he replied sarcastically. 'The
money will grow so fast that you will be unable to count it. By
the way, who involved you into the business?'

'Don't you see?' Kennedy said showing him a carton
of many letters from various companies appealing to him to
join business. 'I can't say how they knew I, a black man, could
be viable for shares.'

Foti laughed, walking again towards the window. This time Ken was annoyed because his father seemed be mocking at him.

'My son, this is a blind investment. This is the beginning of the end.'

At the time they were talking, it would not be long before company shareholders, board of directors and its legal representatives would sit for a decisive meeting.

Foti was eager to leave the following day for Switzerland.

Twenty-Two

Just three weeks after Foti left, the case The People of the Republic of Germany vs. PainKi was heard for a second time. Claimants seemed to be breaking even and the court placed an injunction order on PainKi. All activities were suspended until further notice.

The management of the company summoned all shareholders and the manager of Corksa for an extraordinary meeting the proceeding day.

Corksa was a company producing small bottles, corks and other related products. It had contracted to supply small bottles to PainKi for a period of three years. PainKi was their highest consumer at this time. Because of the crisis, there was imminent close down of Corksa, which was also heavily claimed in court for environmental pollution.

The following morning, the emergency meeting started. The general manager addressed some few issues and the board of directors started listening to shareholders.

Kennedy was the fourth speaker. In a typical African style, he stood and clapped hands as a form of respect. It seemed strange. A typical German would sit down comfortably while talking.

'I think you are all aware in this meeting that not every shareholder understands German,' Kennedy said. Everybody grumbled.

'Mr. Kennedy Foti,' said the manager, 'we are sorry you joined this business at the very moment it is facing a serious quagmire. However, we are twisting things to liquidate the company and to change the name and line of business. You will be informed of any other decision taken. You are in Germany and that obliges you to learn and be able to speak German.'

This intimidated him. He looked at his watch, adjusted it on his wrist and shook his head in distress. He left the meeting with many questions he had prepared to ask and without understanding any decision that was taken in the meeting.

There was a sense of serious manipulation. He entered his car and his head fell on the steering wheel. Things were becoming cruel, he thought.

'My Dad said this,' he thought. He saw another shareholder entering his car. 'Cruel serpents,' he said venomously as he drove off.

Night returned. Kennedy was sitting with his head on the table and his hands on his knees. It was a detestable moment.

'Better to walk comfortably in your shoes than fly uncomfortably on another man's plane,' he said to himself. He was feeling pains all over his body. He walked to the window and looked around. There was nothing to rekindle him.

Someone soon rang at the door. He looked at the clock. It was 10 pm. Katherine entered.

She had wished to know his source of money, but he had blasted her on several occasions. What's more, his father had also shouted on her on several occasions because she used to pick Kennedy's calls.

When she entered, she didn't greet him but went directly to the bedroom and put on her nightgown. When she walked to the sitting room, she asked, 'Why are you like this?' He was quiet. 'I hope I have done nothing wrong this time because you blame me for everything these days.'

Still, he was quiet. She soothed his hair and added, 'You are behaving like a woman.' Kennedy exploded.

'Woman, walk out of here. Go out of this house now and leave me to face my problems alone.'

Katherine dressed and banged the door but in two minutes, she rang again. He neglected it. She did it several times. He walked to the door and opened it. 'Let it not be that you are mad. What do you want?'

'What is the problem, Ken? Are you alright this night?'

'Woman, I have asked you to leave. Is that clear?'

Katherine left peacefully. She wasn't that kind of a nagging woman. After all, she wasn't too desperate for the relationship because he had started behaving strangely, although she had wanted they were married.

Twenty-Three

Three months later, Foti sort asylum and was issued a temporary resident permit. He was disappointed in his son and didn't want to call him often as used to be.

He was assigned an asylum room in a small village, some two kilometres from Lesley city where he had asked for refuge. The same week he received his permit, he went to BIB for advice on how to withdraw some money and to also maintain his membership with BIB. He was asked to come with all necessary documents including his passport before the least word could be spoken.

There were many mix-ups. He thought he could involve a lawyer to facilitate withdrawals. Was it easy? He had still to know more about the institution he was involved in.

* * * *

Switzerland and BIB banking had evolved over the years. When Foti first came to Switzerland to establish an account, Batholo made considerable findings about BIB.

In the evening, they sat at Batholo's. They were eating fried chicken wings and drinking red South African wine. He licked his index finger and looked at his friend.

'I met a good friend and we discussed about BIB.'

'When was that?' asked Foti with much concern.

'The last time you came here.'

'Yes, what is special?'

'You know Switzerland has remained independent in the face of geo-global politics. I was told it is one of the safest places to hide money but at the same time, it could be hard to withdraw.'

'I don't understand what you mean. If it could be hard to withdraw, then how safe is it? I think you don't know much about BIB.'

He didn't want his friend to discourage him.

'Do you know USA is pressurising Switzerland to abolish their banking secrets? According to USA, Switzerland should be open in the way they deal in banking.'

Foti sipped wine and his face wrinkled. 'Do you know how many EU countries are appealing to join them? USA is just a power monger country. It wants to be the world power in everything.'

'How are you going to make withdrawals without any papers or cards?'

'That is where the problem lies.'

The following day, he took a shower earlier than used to be. By five he was already fresh and was looking at his watch expecting it to tick to 8.30 am. BIB would open at nine that morning up to four in the evening.

At 8.45 am he dropped from the train. From the Lesley train station, he could see the edifice. It was indeed a huge tower. At the top of it was written BIB. Under that was written again in black ink, *WORLD SAFEST BANK*. He descended from the train station with his heart beating abnormally.

It was about five minutes to the hour of nine. He stood a few metres away watching the structure and waiting for the offices to open.

A group of architects designed the glittering limestone supper structure. Its construction started several years back and completion took place in the year 2000.

The main metal door of BIB suddenly divided into two halves and each side slid into the wall. Through the main door, the first room was the reception.

There were other doors at the other three sides of the building. These were for customers who wished to go directly to various dispensers for transactions within Switzerland. However, any transaction that was international and concerning foreign nationals was directed to the reception.

Foti was the first customer at the reception. A tall slim man in a sober suit stood near a table sipping hot coffee.

When he saw Foti approaching, he pushed it aside and said, 'Good morning, Sir. How can I help you?'

'I am Foti Posh, Sir.'

'Yes, Sir,' answered the man ready to help him.

'I am a customer and would like to have a talk on how to make withdrawals.'

The man hurried up to usher him to a corner where there was a set of cushion chairs. As he was doing so, he frowned and doubted. Perhaps he thought how a customer of their bank could be asking means of withdrawals. However, he said, 'Can you sit down here, Sir?'

'Thank you.'

'Yes. I am listening to you, Sir.'

'Hmmm, emmm… I have an account here and I wish to follow up for necessary transfers and withdrawals.'

The man looked at him and shifted his chair closer.

'I can't really make a point. Do you have a BIB account?'

'Yes, Sir.'

'And you want to withdraw or transfer some money?'

'Yes, Sir.'

'Can I see your bank card or account booklet?'

'I don't have any, Sir. I have left everything back home.'

'Which home?'

'I am a Cameroonian, and I have all documents there.'

'How can you come for money transaction without necessary documents? Can I see your passport? Maybe it's going to help check your account.'

He hesitated for seconds before taking out his Swiss temporary resident permit. The man starred at it. His head was moving from the small piece of paper to Foti's face and back to it. There was totally no comprehension.

'This is a temporary resident permit from council authorities.'

'Yes, Sir. I have applied for political asylum here. Before then, I established an account with this bank but it is rather unfortunate that I have left all papers back home.'

'Ok, Mr. Foti, come with me.'

He took him to the next room. 'Mr. Blatt, there is a case here that needs your attention.'

He handed him over to Blatt, explained what was going on and left for the reception. Blatt was there to handle complicated matters. From his face, it seemed he hated to smile. He was a grey man with fallen jaws. He studied the paper and asked, 'You mean you have political problems back home and can't have your papers? Is that what you mean?'

'Yes, Sir.'

'Really, I doubt your identity. I am afraid this piece of paper doesn't qualify you, nor does it convince me to even check our computers to verify any information. I am sorry.'

'What do you mean?' Foti asked as he heaved backwards. 'I have a huge sum in this bank, Sir.'

'That is not the bone of contention. The point is that we can't release somebody's account information to you.'

'Somebody...?'

'Yes. I can only tell you to seek legal advice. We have nothing to offer you.'

He handed the paper to him and expected him to leave. Foti sat still, thinking of what to say. 'Please, do something, Sir.'

'You are getting disturbing now. I suggest you leave now!'

'What if I can't have the papers at the end of it all?'

'Why not?'

'I don't think I will go back to my country sooner or later.'

'Did you kill somebody? Why can't you go back to your country? Please, just leave now.'

It was total disillusionment. He walked out of the building with hatred. About fifty metres away from it, he turned and looked at the luxurious structure. 'What does this really mean?' he asked himself.

At this time, he only thought of Vincent Omotula, a popular and able lawyer. Someone had given him his address to consult for legal advice before he even applied for asylum. Lawyer Omotula was known for winning cases for many Africans.

'My lawyer will challenge the idiots in court,' he said to himself.

At home, he didn't want to think that all was lost. He called Omotula and they made a rendezvous that same week on Friday.

Twenty-Four

Fridays were days most lawyers would spend in their offices. Court sessions were often held from Monday to Thursday weekly. That morning, Omotula was expecting Foti.

He was one of the few blacks practicing in Switzerland. His parents brought him there when he was ten, and they were all granted asylum. Though faced with tough racism, he fought hard to become a lawyer.

Omotula had fought together with the World Bank for the stolen funds hidden by a Nigerian former president's son in a Swiss bank to be returned. He hated the way African leaders were siphoning massive sums and dumping them in western banks.

When Foti rang, the secretary opened. Omotula was in his office sipping hot coffee. She spoke with him briefly on phone and immediately directed Foti there. When Foti entered, he pushed the cup aside and greeted him.

'Good morning. How are you doing?'

'Fine, Sir.'

'Have a seat.'

'Thanks.'

'Can I help you?'

'Yes, Sir.'

He presented to him his identification paper. The lawyer looked at it.

'You have a problem and you want me to help you, is that?'

'Yes, Sir.'

When he started searching for a file to take down his case, Foti raised his head to the wall. He saw the picture of the lawyer in legal robes with some judges wearing frightful wigs. The first thing that came to his mind was when he used to buy off lawyers and judges in criminal cases in which he was involved.

'Ok, Mr. Fooo… What is your name again?' he asked picking up the piece of paper to read the name.

'Ok, Mr. Foti Posh,' he read out the name as written on the small piece of paper.

'Right, Sir,' Foti confirmed.

'Let me hear you now.'

Foti explained all details. The barrister was puzzled. When he asked him to explain a second time, Foti thought he had a good lawyer who could fight for him. When he finished, the lawyer folded his arms and breathed heavily.

'Mr. Foti, can you tell me how much you have in the said account? Just tell me the amount again.'

'Five hundred million francs CFA.'

'That is in Cameroon currency.'

'Yes, Sir.'

'Don't tell me that. You said you were a mayor. What other business were you doing? Do you own a company?'

'No, Sir.'

'How many children do you have?'

'Three.'

'A wife?'

'Yes, Sir.'

'Where are they now?'

'One is in Germany, and the other two with my wife are in the US.'

'I can't really understand. In fact, just tell me why you decided to block this kind of huge sum in a western bank.'

Foti frowned and was almost getting annoyed.

'Well, I don't mean to dissuade you in any way, Foti.'

'If you say so.'

'Why didn't you keep this money in any bank in your country? You decided to bring it here. Is there electricity in your village? Does your village have good drinking water?'

Foti wasn't ready to talk any more. He was nervous and ready to leave. When he stayed quiet for about two minutes, Omotula said venomously, 'Walk out of my office.'

He immediately fell out and disappeared into the streets.

Twenty-Five

Foti screamed daily. He was in serious pains. For several weeks, he didn't eat but would drink more than a fish from morning until evening. He was seeking solace in alcohol bottles.

Several years back, his physician had warned him to stay away from alcohol because of heart problems. This time, the problem could double because he was drinking spirits on an empty stomach. He became so fragile and appeared hopeless.

Since the day he left BIB, Batholo was able to meet him just once. On other occasions he came and rang, Foti didn't want to open his door. He seemed frustrated and was ready to die. His life changed.

Batholo didn't know how to arrest the situation. He succeeded to reach Kennedy and explained all that was happening. Ken decided to drive from Germany to see his father that weekend, and Batholo wanted to seize the opportunity to see how his friend was coping with the situation.

Twenty-Six

It was 5.45 pm and Batholo was there at the train station expecting to receive Kennedy driving all the way from Germany. It wasn't long before he arrived. For him, there was still some hope because he still had some money left in the bank. His father could as well manage life from the same account. However, he was completely a greedy man who never wanted to deal with chicken feed.

He had refused talking to his son each time he called. On his own part, his son had thought his anger was about the fact that he took shares in a company without any advice.

From the station, they drove direct to his father. They rang for more than five minutes but it seemed no one was there.

'Do you think my Dad is alive?'

'Why not? These shoes seem to have been used today,' said Batholo pointing at slippers near the door. Kennedy looked at them closely. There was all indication that he was around. He approached a woman who was standing by and seemed to be a neighbour.

'Good evening, Madame,' he greeted.

'Thanks. Good evening too.'

'Do you know the person living in this apartment?'

'Yes, but not so much.'

'Have you seen him today?'

'Yes. I saw him there at the door sitting. It seems he is a patient. Is that?'

'No. Not really.'

'I know him. He has a scraggy structure.'

Kennedy was afraid when the woman said he was skinny. They turned back to the door and rang heavily hitting it at the same time. Still, there was no sign of any human life at that moment.

'Ken,' proposed Batholo, 'let us inform the police.'

Kennedy stood for some time thinking. 'Something is telling me that my father is in here. I will break this door now. It is not made of hard wood.'

'It is against the law. Only the police can do that.' Kennedy didn't want to waste any time.

He smashed it forcefully with his leg twice and it opened. From outside, they saw Foti leaning and in a deep sleep. In his left hand was a bottle of vodka and in his right, a key. His eyes were closed. Kennedy's eyes rushed round the whole room and back to his father. He walked closer.

'Is he alive? Dad!' he yelled trying to shake him.

It immediately occurred to Batholo that Foti was dead when he touched his forehead but he didn't want to express it. When they shook him heavily and there was no reaction, Kennedy shouted, 'My father is dead! Oh, God, help me!'

Batholo immediately called the police with his mobile telephone. Later, an ambulance arrived. They rushed him to the nearest hospital. The police had informed the doctors while the ambulance was still on the way. Three doctors were at the door seriously waiting. They rushed Foti in and within ten minutes, the doctor told Kennedy that his father had died some five hours before. Two hours later, the doctors said the immediate cause of his death was cardiac arrest.